MW00532312

Hadley wrote d⸱ went slack when sh⸱ message. "Tell him ⸱ ⸱⸱⸱⸱⸱⸱⸱⸱⸱ ⸱ ⸱⸱⸱⸱⸱⸱⸱⸱⸱ ⸱⸱⸱⸱⸱⸱⸱⸱⸱. It's urgent."

A shot of adrenalin coursed through Hadley's veins. Sandro Botticelli. Her favorite artist in the whole world. Creator of the Italian masterpiece, Nascita di Venere, The Birth of Venus, the ancient Goddess of Love, dated circa 1484. She wasn't aware a Botticelli painting was missing.

"Is there any additional information you can give me? The name of the painting? The provenance? Capito. I understand the need for utmost secrecy. We can set up a meeting, and I'll make sure Signore Domingo will be there."

She jotted down some more notes. "Piazzale Michelangelo? At sunset?"

Hadley tilted her head and chewed on her bottom lip. That was a strange destination for a business meeting. Although it offered the most scenic view of the city, perched atop a hillside overlooking Florence, meeting at a park after dark was reminiscent of a murder scene in a film noir. Where the heroine, Hadley, would later be found, dead, her virtue compromised and her throat slit. She would have to get Luca to drive her up on his motorcycle and stay out of sight while she conducted her business.

Was the female caller from a museum? A high-end gallery? An auction house? Was she an art or antiquities dealer, or a wealthy private individual, or was she representing a government agency? And, if so, which government? Enemy or ally? She would soon find out.

Praise for Marilyn Baron

"*THE ROMANOV LEGACY: A NOVEL* is…historical fiction shrouded in mystery and intrigue…an unbelievable story amongst historical fact [set in] the lavish world of Imperial Russia, …secret societies, carrying on the bloodlines, and unraveling a puzzle."

~*NN Light's Book Heaven (5 Stars)*

"*STUMBLE STONES*…named so for the plaques laid in tribute to victims of the Holocaust, possesses the best qualities of historical romance. Baron knows her settings and her history, and her characters…are well-drawn and convincing."

~*Georgia Author of the Year Judge*

"*THE ALIBI*…Southern, small town mystery, intrigue, suspense, murder, and a bit of down-home charm. …and an absolute enjoyable read."

~*Gabrielle Sally, The Romance Reviews (5 Stars)*

"A compelling and entertaining story…a superb job with character[s]…the story fun and enticing!"

~*Turning Another Page, Book Unleashed (5 Stars)*

"Marilyn Baron brings a unique style to her quirky and fast-paced stories that keeps readers turning pages."

~*New York Times Bestseller Dianna Love*

"A treasure trove of mystery and intrigue…."

~*Andrew Kirby*

STRACCIATELLA GELATO: MELTING TIME

"A quick and fantastical read…traveling back to a special time or… place…in our hearts and minds…"

~*Laura Hartland (5 Stars)*

"Fast, enjoyable read…has gotten me in the mood to read again. Thanks to the author for that gift."

~*GerriP (5 Stars)*

The Case of the Missing Botticelli

and

The Case of the Vanishing Vermeer

by
Marilyn Baron

Two Massimo Domingo Mysteries

The Case of the Missing Botticelli and The Case of the Vanishing Vermeer

Cover Art by *Debbie Taylor*

The Wild Rose Press, Inc.
PO Box 708
Adams Basin, NY 14410-0708
Visit us at www.thewildrosepress.com

Publishing History
First Edition, 2022
Trade Paperback ISBN 978-1-5092-3970-2
Digital ISBN 978-1-5092-3971-9

Two Massimo Domingo Mysteries
Published in the United States of America

Dedication

I dedicate this book to my wonderful daughters,
Marissa and Amanda, and to my granddaughter, Aviva.

Part One
The Case of the Missing Botticelli

"Researching a lost work of art is like solving a mystery—and, as is often the case, sometimes the mystery is only partially unraveled, while threads of other mysteries are discovered."
~from "Researching the Lost Portrait of Gutle Rothschild," a December 1, 2020, Hadassah-Brandeis Institute blog by Dr. Susan Nashman Fraiman, a researcher and curator of Jewish and Israeli art, about a painting by Moritz Oppenheim

Chapter One

Firenze (Florence), Italy

"Pronto."

Hadley Evans finished sipping her fizzy lemon soda, savoring the satisfying blend of tart and sweet tastes on her tongue and the sparkling slide of the cold liquid down her throat. Setting the drink aside on her desk, she picked up a pen and a pink telephone message pad.

"Signore Domingo is not available at the moment. He's at lunch. No, I don't know when he'll be back."

The caller's impatient tone bled through the telephone line, piercing Hadley's already super-frayed nerve endings. Her boss was dining on a back street at Trattoria La Strada around the corner from Santa Felicita Church. The trattoria was where all the locals dined. Fridays were typically crowded and packed with Fiorentinos and tourists who came to ogle the statue of David, swoon over the paintings in the Uffizi, load up on leather goods, gorge on cups of rich gelato, and shop for gold and jewelry in the high-end shops along the Ponte Vecchio. The restaurant was not much to look at on the outside, but inside, the smells and the cuisine were divine, courtesy of the owner's parents, who doubled as the chefs. Which is why any Italian worth his buffalo mozzarella dined there.

Signore Domingo was on the portly side because

eating pasta was his favorite pastime. He'd already been gone two hours, so he was most definitely lingering over dessert. If Hadley had to guess, right about now, he'd be ordering the special tiramisu of the day and playing footsies under the table with his latest innamorata—Simonetta or Angelina or Sophia—the current flavor of the week.

"I'll be glad to take a message. No, I'm not the secretary. She's out. I'm just covering for her. I'm Signore Domingo's assistant." Nothing wrong with a little white lie. She was actually Signore Domingo's gofer. For the last six months, he'd kept her dashing around Florence running errands, like picking up his laundry, keeping his office stocked with sweet and savory snacks, making restaurant reservations, and shopping for gifts for his wife to keep her off the scent of his mistress-a-la-mode. So not exactly what she signed up for when she took the job.

Although she was hoping for some additional responsibility, running errands only made her fall more in love with Florence. There were no malls or big supermarkets. If she wanted a quart of milk, she could walk into the corner coffee bar. If she craved something sweet, she could visit a secret bakery shop for a hot, fresh pastry or wander to the local florist where she was greeted like a friend by the flower lady when she picked up a fragrant bouquet. The gourmet food court at *Mercato Centrale* offered the region's best wines and local ingredients.

She enjoyed the personalized service and the intimate relationship with the people who sold her things—from fragrance to fashion. The familiar sights and sounds and smells. And the priceless artwork on display in the museums around the city—the Uffizi, the Bargello, the Academia, and the treasures tourists so often miss—hidden away in the churches.

She knew her way around every narrow street and alleyway. Her heart swelled at the sounds of the church bells in the religious center, as she walked in the shadow of the traditional Florentine tower houses in the heart of Florence's historical center and on to the medieval quarter to the political center of the city. She paused for refreshment at Government Square, Piazza Signoria, with its statues, the sculptures in the Loggia, the monuments that made Florence the destination for some eleven million tourists a year.

She'd been told she could almost pass for an Italian—with her thick and lustrous, long and wavy auburn hair, green eyes, and a girl-next-door smile, until she opened her mouth. Then her accent gave her away as a foreigner. Fake it till you make it wasn't exactly working for her.

She was living la dolce vita. But as her mother and father reminded her every weekend when they talked, she was living in a dream world and did she understand that one day she was going to have to come home and face reality? Start her actual life? Marry her college sweetheart? Have children? Did she realize there were plenty of museums in America? And coming home didn't include bringing home an Italian boyfriend to meet the parents.

She had moved to the city to finish her degree in Art History from Florida State University on the Florence Program. After graduation, program director Dr. Franco Dotti had graciously arranged for a job interview. He'd touted Signore Domingo's stellar reputation as an art detective, a rather obscure but fascinating profession, and his great respect for art history. She knew she wanted to stay in Florence as long as possible to bathe in the Birthplace of the Renaissance and stay close to Luca, the sexy cop she was dating, a member of the Carabinieri, one of Italy's national police forces. She and Luca were from opposite sides of the world, yet they spoke a common language—not Italian—the language of love. Well, not love exactly, more the lust she experienced when she gazed into his big brown eyes and the rugged planes and angles of his handsome face and when he kissed her and held her against his sturdy body. So, for the moment, she was willing to work for paltry wages.

She and Luca weren't at the serious stage, but she loved being with him. She wasn't planning to marry him, of course. He hadn't even introduced her to his parents. Eventually, she'd return to the States and marry her acceptable-to-her-mother longtime boyfriend King Charles. His actual name was Charles King, but once he'd shown her an email—an acceptance letter from law school that had addressed him as King, Charles. And although she never referred to him by that name to his face, the nickname stuck.

When she'd last seen King Charles, he was enrolled in law school. But then she'd received an email from her best frenemy delightfully revealing that he had dropped out of law school and was riding the campus bus, counting students. He never told her he had quit law school and she never told him about Luca. So much for honest relationships. King Charles had been promising to fly over and visit her one of these days, but the days rolled into weeks and the weeks into months, and loneliness and homesickness had set in and messed with her mind.

She spent the first few months of her college program down in the basement of the hotel that housed the students, missing King Charles, drowning her sorrows in cheap wine, and crying over "It Don't Matter to Me," "Baby I'm-A Want You," and "Diary," and the soft melodies of America, singing "I Need You," with some classic rock thrown in, the more melancholy, the better.

When King Charles wrote her that he wouldn't be flying to Florence to spend her summer vacation traveling around Europe, she hitchhiked to Rome and hooked up with Trace, a tall American tourist from Texas, where after an exhausting day of sightseeing, they ended up sharing a bottle of Chianti and a bed. Was it because he was an American and she knew she'd never see him again?

And was that why, when on a ski trip to Zermatt, Switzerland, she'd slept with the son of a colonel from the air force base in Pisa because she'd had too much Sambuca or because, when she visited the base, they offered barbecues? And, after a steady diet of pasta, she was ready to do almost anything for a hamburger.

And was that why she had held out for so long before sleeping with Luca, because he wasn't American?

She hadn't set out to cheat on King Charles, but as far as she was concerned their relationship was in limbo. Then she met Luca, under rather unusual circumstances. As a student in a foreign country, she had been walking to class in the streets along with the rest of the crowd, and suddenly someone yelled, "Jump!" Naturally, she jumped to her right toward the sidewalk and collided with a young man on a motorcycle. Luca was the cop who ticketed her and took her to the police station where she was charged with "walking in the streets" and had to pay for the damage to the boy's bike.

"Are you seriously arresting me?" Hadley had protested.

"I'm just following the law."

"You were walking in the street, and so was everyone else," she'd objected.

"Do you always do what everyone else does?"

Hadley fumed.

"And I didn't knock over a man on a motorbike and damage his property," Luca maintained.

"It was an accident. And he hit *me*, an innocent pedestrian."

"Who should have been walking on the sidewalk. The law is the law."

"Are you always so unyielding?"

"Yes, when I'm right."

"And are you always right?"

"Usually."

"Do me a favor. If you ever see me on the street, don't talk to me. Pretend you don't know me, *capito*?"

Luca's face spread into a smile.

"Are you laughing at me?"

"No, just your accent. You make *capito* sound like it rhymes with libido."

Mad as she was at him, he had served as her translator and insisted on helping her through the process. The biker wanted her to meet him in a park at night and hand over the damages to fix his motorbike in cash. Luca instructed her not to go. The biker continued to harass her until one day the calls stopped. Hadley had spoken to her parents, who told her their insurance policy had paid him the $15,000 for damages to his bike.

A few days later, she ran into Luca and his dog in the park. The dog jumped up, placed his paws on her breasts and attempted to tackle her to the ground. She got down on her haunches and started playing with him.

"Oh, you're so cute. What's your name?"

"It's Bocelli," Luca said.

"After Andrea Bocelli?"

"Yes."

"He's my favorite singer."

"Mine too. I'm Luca, by the way."

"I know who you are," she said with a sideways glance.

"You said the next time we meet I was to pretend I didn't know you, so I'm reintroducing myself."

Then he had the nerve to ask her out on a date. She didn't want to go at first, she was so mad at the Carabinieri and their silly laws and the fact that her parents' insurance company had to pay because someone on a motorbike hit her. If anyone should have sued, it should have been her. But Luca's good looks, charm and, oh, yes, the way he filled out his uniform, won the day. When he said something in Italian that sounded like, "Love my dog, love me," she melted. In the end he wore down her resistance, like an unsuspecting frog, slowly boiling in a pot, that didn't realize it was in hot water. By the time she knew it, she was in his bed. Possibly it was lust that drew him to her initially. She wasn't sure she should trust her emotions.

Since she'd shown up on Signore Domingo's office doorstep, he hadn't trusted her with a real assignment, which she was perfectly capable of handling. What she didn't know then but she knew now, was that Signore

Domingo was living on his laurels, along with multiple daily helpings of pasta, that he hadn't caught a decent case in years, and that, after half a year in his employ, she was no closer to her ultimate goal of becoming a museum curator or director.

While in college in Florence, she had attended art history, Italian, literature, and mythology classes during the week and spent weekends traveling around Europe with other students on the program. Her first stop in any new city was always the local art museum, whereas her friends frequently made a beeline for the trendiest bars and the best beer festivals.

****

Hadley rubbed her eyes, trying to stave off a headache while she continued her telephone conversation with the unidentified woman.

"Of course you can trust me. I promise I will pass on this message and your phone number as soon as Signore Domingo walks in the door."

Hadley wrote down the phone number, and her jaw went slack when she heard and inscribed the rest of the message. "Tell him it's about a missing Botticelli. It's urgent."

A shot of adrenalin coursed through Hadley's veins. Sandro Botticelli. Her favorite artist in the whole world. Creator of the Italian masterpiece, *Nascita di Venere*, *The Birth of Venus*, the ancient Goddess of Love, dated circa 1484. She wasn't aware a Botticelli painting was missing.

"Is there any additional information you can give me? The name of the painting? The provenance? *Capito*. I understand the need for utmost secrecy. We can set up a meeting, and I'll make sure Signore Domingo will be

8

there."

She jotted down some more notes. "Piazzale Michelangelo? At sunset?"

Hadley tilted her head and chewed on her bottom lip. That was a strange destination for a business meeting. Although it offered the most scenic view of the city, perched atop a hillside overlooking Florence, meeting at a park after dark was reminiscent of a murder scene in a film noir. Where the heroine, Hadley, would later be found, dead, her virtue compromised and her throat slit. She would have to get Luca to drive her up on his motorcycle and stay out of sight while she conducted her business.

Was the female caller from a museum? A high-end gallery? An auction house? Was she an art or antiquities dealer, or a wealthy private individual, or was she representing a government agency? And, if so, which government? Enemy or ally? She would soon find out.

Was it advisable to go to a park at night? Definitely not. The woman could be representing a client from the criminal art world. That's why Luca had to accompany her. She intended to sweet-talk him into helping her. After all, he was in line to become a detective. He was used to investigations. He'd welcome the practice. And above all, Luca was a protector. It was inbred in him.

"You're staying at L'Hotel Bernini Palace?"

That explained it. The five-star hotel was near the Piazzale. So, a high-end client. Just what the firm needed.

"He'll be there," Hadley assured.

Hadley held the message in her quivering hand, pursed her lips, then stashed it in her new Furla handbag. What if the message had somehow been unintentionally misplaced without Signore Domingo seeing it, and she contrived to meet the contact alone? Once her boss saw she could solve a case on her own, he would finally bring her into the fold and teach her secrets of the art theft underworld she was so desperate to learn.

She already knew the basics. On her first day at the office, he'd proudly given her a copy of his book, "Massimo Domingo's Pocket Guide to Stolen Art Recovery—Volume I." There hadn't been a Volume II. Signore Domingo hadn't gotten around to writing it. But she was sure there was a lot more information and wisdom he had to impart. She was ready to soak up his knowledge like a sponge, but so far all he'd told her was, "It's all in the book."

The phone rang again.

"Massimo Domingo Art Detective Agency."

She listened to a tourist drone on about how she wanted to bring back a memento from her romantic trip to Florence, expressing her interest in buying a painting to fulfill that desire.

"No, we're not an art gallery. We don't sell paintings, we retrieve them."

Hadley sighed. She recommended the Giuseppe Zocchi Gallery on The Piazza della Signoria. Too bad she wasn't working on commission.

The phone rang again.

"Massimo Domingo Art Detective Agency. No, this is not a museum. We are an art detective agency. We locate lost paintings and return them to their legal or rightful owners. But have you been to the Uffizi Gallery?" She might as well be working for a tourist agency.

Hadley slipped off her kitten-heeled shoes and

massaged her aching feet. Where was Gerda? She should have been back from her doctor's appointment by now.

Looking around the well-appointed office, decorated with the loving touch of Signora Domingo, Massimo's wife, her eyes wandered to the Signore's favorite print. It was labeled, "*Arte per amore dell'arte*," or Art for Art's Sake. A similar poster was displayed in the office window. Signore Massimo Domingo was a big player in the art world, or at least he had been. According to Gerda, his longtime and long-suffering German secretary, in his heyday he was well respected and prominent. But now she referred to him behind his back as a has-been, an also-ran.

"The Poor Rachmanus."

Gerda labeled almost everyone in need of mercy, compassion, or pity a "Poor Rachmanus."

Earlier that morning, Hadley had asked Gerda how Signore Domingo was able to afford the rent and pay their salaries with no visible work coming in.

"Family money, specifically his *wife's* family money, and he does it because he loves art."

"Sorry I'm late," Gerda apologized, sailing into the office. "There were so many people in the waiting room." Gerda was short in stature, with curly, dark hair, a pillowy bosom, and a pleasant face that belied her caustic wit. She ran the office like a drill sergeant. She had organizational skills General George S. Patton could only dream of.

"Is everything okay?" Hadley asked.

"Just routine. Did anything happen while I was gone?" Then she let out a belly laugh. "Of course it didn't. Nothing important ever happens around here."

"Just the usual wrong numbers." Hadley flushed,

remembering the cryptic message burning a hole in her handbag. She didn't tell Gerda about the mysterious phone call and the missing Botticelli painting. She was determined to solve this case on her own to prove her value, to bring in an income stream for the firm, perhaps enhance its reputation. This was her big chance. She would tell the potential client that Signore Domingo was tied up (which, depending on his sexual proclivities, could possibly be true), and that as his most trusted assistant, she would be handling the case. She would present the woman with a fait accompli.

"When do you think the boss will get back from La Strada's?" Hadley asked.

Gerda howled with laughter. "How long has he been gone?"

"Two hours."

"Well, don't expect him back today. It's Friday. He is quite infatuated with his latest conquest. Simonetta is her name, I think. I imagine they'll be occupied for the rest of the afternoon."

The buzzer rang, and in walked a disheveled middle-aged man, with a hunchback, in a wrinkled trench coat. He wandered over to Gerda's desk. "Do you sell art supplies here?"

Gerda rolled her eyes. "No, this isn't an art supply shop."

"But the poster in the window says, 'Art For Art's Sake.'"

Gerda stashed her purse in her desk drawer and sighed loudly.

"That's just a phrase," she explained patiently. "It means that art needs no justification except for the love and appreciation of art for its own sake."

Hadley took pity on the man, probably a starving artist, and recommended Castle Art's on Via Federico Grifeo.

"Sorry to have bothered you." Dejected, he walked slowly out the door.

"The Poor Rachmanus," Gerda said, shaking her head.

Hadley walked by Gerda's desk and through her boss's office door to hang his laundry in the wardrobe. Normally his wife handled the laundry, but Hadley took charge when there were lipstick stains on the collars of his shirts. While there, she opened Massimo's desk drawer, slipping a black address book with the Signore's Italian, European, and international contacts into her skirt pocket. Just another dive into a clandestine cesspool. In the drawer, she also found an olive-oil-stained copy of "Massimo Domingo's Pocket Guide to Stolen Art Recovery." She carried out the copy along with a large scrapbook that took pride of place on the Signore's cluttered desk.

"Do you think the Signore would mind if I borrow his copy of the *Pocket Guide*? My copy is at home."

Gerda laughed. "I have a thousand more copies gathering dust in a storage unit."

"I thought he said it was a bestseller."

"Maybe in some obscure genre like Clichéd Stolen Art Recovery Pocket Guides."

"Well, then, how—"

"His wife bought up all the copies. He doesn't know. The Poor Rachmanus."

"Do you think Signore Domingo would mind if I looked through his scrapbook?"

"I don't see why not," Gerda said. "He's very proud

of everything he's accomplished. He spent his life tracking down the world's great stolen masterpieces, from Donatellos to daVincis, Rembrandt van Rijns to Vincent Van Goghs."

Hadley spread the album out on her desk and began looking through the press clippings. The book documented page after page of Signore Domingo's early successes, his glory days when the denizens of the art world whispered its secrets to the "confessor" about dozens of stolen works of art, tip-offs that enabled him to track down multi-million-dollar masterpieces. The Signore, twenty kilos lighter in his pictures, looked dapper, self-assured, and happy.

She couldn't imagine anyone confessing or whispering to Signore Domingo today or the Signore chasing down anyone but his current and erstwhile mistresses around his bedroom. The Signore had even been involved with trying to track the thieves from the 1990 Isabella Stewart Gardner Museum case in Boston, history's biggest art heist. To date, no one had found those pieces. Now, according to Gerda, he was the Inspector Clouseau of the art world. He made his living mostly from his spotty art consultancy practice.

"Why do you stay with him?" Hadley wondered.

"Because, back in the day, he was really something." The way she said it, with a gleam in her eye, suggested there might have once been something between them or at least that she had harbored feelings for her boss. But they acted like colleagues in the office, nothing more.

"Gerda?" Hadley inquired, choked with doubt and guilt. "If we did have a client who needed to get in touch with the Signore, should I disturb him?"

"Not unless you want to get fired. Signora Domingo is out of town, so he would have taken his mistress home, and they'll be indisposed the entire weekend."

"What if it was an important case?"

"Doubtful. Just handle it yourself, then. You'll never get anywhere around here if you don't take the initiative."

Just then, a short, trim, stylish, middle-aged blonde strolled into the shop.

"Gerda, Hadley, how are you today?"

Gerda's eyes widened.

"S-Signora D-Domingo, this is unexpected," Gerda stuttered. "I thought you were visiting relatives in Rome, that you wouldn't be back until Sunday."

"I came home early to surprise my husband. I thought we'd take a stroll down the Arno River like we used to. Is Massimo in his office?"

Gerda shot Hadley a panicked look. Sensing Gerda's distress, Hadley weighed in.

"The Signore had an important case that just came up at the last minute. He was called away to the um, Art Squad, I believe."

The Signora smiled. "How wonderful. I've been worried about Massimo lately. He seems despondent, worried about something. I thought it might be a midlife crisis, but I'm glad things are going well at the office."

"I, um, have just picked up some of his laundry, if you want to take that home," Hadley managed. "I don't believe he's coming back into the office today." She walked into her boss's office and carried the laundered shirts back to the Signora.

"Thank you, Hadley. You shouldn't be doing this. That's my job. You should be working on more important things."

Ya think?

"It was no trouble," Hadley said. "Signore Domingo has been very busy these days. I'm glad to help out."

"And how's that handsome young man of yours?" Signora Domingo asked, smiling.

"Luca is fine, thank you."

"He works for the Carabinieri, doesn't he?"

"Yes."

"That's wonderful. Remember these times. Being young and in love." The Signora stared off into the distance with a dreamy, faraway look. "I see you're looking at my husband's scrapbook. My, he was a good-looking man, wasn't he?"

"Yes," Hadley agreed. Massimo had been handsome in the day, but his chiseled good looks and lanky frame were now more fleshy than flattering. Obviously, the Signora was in the "more of him to love" camp.

"Well, I'd best be getting home to make dinner before Massimo returns. It was wonderful to see you both."

As soon as the Signora left the office, Gerda, Massimo's apologist, swore, "*Scheisse!*"

"Do you think she suspects anything?" Hadley asked, crinkling her nose.

"No, the Poor Rachmanus. She doesn't have a devious bone in her body. She's a saint. She has to be to put up with our boss."

Gerda dialed Massimo's number and pursed her lips. "Massimo," she chided under her breath. "Pick up your phone."

"He doesn't answer his home phone," Gerda reported. "I'll leave a message on his cell."

"Do you think he's with his mistress?"

"Of course he is. It's Friday, isn't it? If that poor woman comes home and finds him in bed with Simonetta, there will be hell to pay—for all of us.

"Massimo. Your *wife* just stopped in to *surprise* you at the office. She's on her way home, *now!*"

Gerda shook her head. "I don't know how that woman puts up with him."

"She seems very sweet."

"And naïve. But she's in love with him. What can I say? I just hope he gets the message in time."

Hadley sat in the outer office, studying the scrapbook.

Obviously, this mystery client had dealt with the Signore before if she was asking for him personally. Hadley was sure if she perused the old newspaper stories close enough and familiarized herself with the Signore's past cases, she might come up with some clues or leads about the missing Botticelli.

Signore Domingo never admitted to making mistakes. He liked to pontificate, his lectures punctuated by grand hand gestures. Most of his proclamations began, "Did I ever tell you about the time when…" And grousing about how many years it typically took him to crack a case. Or lamenting the ones that got away. She was going to find this missing artwork in record time and salvage the agency's fading reputation.

As a private art crime detective, Massimo Domingo was famous for recovering not only valuable paintings but jewelry, even manuscripts. Often he worked with police. But he was usually the investigator of last resort when police had long given up the search for evidence.

Sometimes he received tips of thefts about to take

place at a museum and he was able to prevent them before the first glass window or door was smashed or sledgehammer wielded. He'd chased leads and followed trails all over the world, and sometimes found priceless paintings hidden in plain sight, hanging in art galleries or on kitchen walls of seaside villas. Or in drug raids or brazenly stolen in art heists from exhibition walls in broad daylight. Often, he'd find them damaged or burned.

But sometimes, they were miraculously recovered and returned either to a museum or the rightful owners from whom they'd been confiscated. That is, if the rightful owners or their heirs were still alive. Many had perished in the Holocaust. Some pieces of art were returned anonymously by thieves who never revealed the location where their stolen paintings had been stashed.

Retrievals were few and far between. The Signore was rarely paid for his expertise, his work was done at his own, or his wife's, expense. He did it for the thrill of chasing leads or chasing headlines—and, yes, for the love of art.

Hadley knew from Signore Domingo that fake art was the third largest criminal activity on the planet and that ten percent of paintings on display in museums were fraudulent. Less than ten percent of those stolen pieces were returned. And it could sometimes take decades before stolen paintings resurfaced.

Sometimes paintings were given to criminals as partial payment for a drug deal. And they could later use those paintings in negotiating immunity or for safekeeping in the event they needed it in the future as collateral or for bargaining, even though a work of art in the criminal underworld was worth only ten percent of its value in the legitimate art market.

She knew that thieves stole paintings primarily for money but then found they couldn't easily sell them on the open market so made them available to other criminals, often for a fraction of their value.

Hadley turned to Gerda and, in the most nonchalant voice she could muster, asked, "Would you mind if I took off next week? Luca and I have plans to ride his motorcycle around the countryside."

"Fine. I'll handle the kooks and the crazies until you get back."

Chapter Two

Luca dropped Hadley off at the edge of the square and drove away on his motorcycle. She strolled toward the designated meeting place, bathed in the lovely evening light, the same light the masters of the Renaissance painted by centuries ago. It was a little cloudy. It had rained that afternoon. There was no one else in sight but a slim, well-dressed woman in her mid-thirties, sporting a dirty-blonde ponytail and a nervous look in her blue eyes.

Hadley was excited about the limitless directions this investigation could take and more than a little anxious about the possible dangers involved, but she was counting on Luca to be there every step of the way. It was the most thrilling thing that had happened to her since she was crowned Little Miss Cheesemonger in third grade in Tallahassee, Florida, in a competition sponsored by Riley's Gourmet Shoppe and Creamery. That was her claim to fame. Her parents still kept the newspaper clipping from the *Tallahassee Observer*.

"Where is Signore Domingo?" the woman demanded, stepping toward her.

"He's been taken ill suddenly. He sent me in his place. I'm his assistant."

"Are you the woman I spoke to this morning on the phone?"

"Yes," said Hadley, projecting an air of confidence

she did not feel.

"I told you this is a very sensitive matter. I will only speak to Signore Domingo."

"Do you know him?"

"Only by reputation."

"I am his right hand. He tells me everything. We work closely together."

"I don't like this. I need to go."

"Wait," said Hadley, placing her hand firmly on the woman's wrist, afraid the client would slip away. "You said it was an urgent matter. I think it best we get right to it."

"How do I know I can trust you? My job, *everything* is on the line. And if this gets out, my reputation is ruined."

"I am very discreet. You've come to the right place. I can help you."

The woman shifted her stance and clutched her designer handbag.

"I'm the new curator at the Uffizi Gallery," the lady began, flexing her hands.

That revelation raised a red flag in Hadley's mind. If this woman worked at the Uffizi Gallery in Florence, then why was she staying at L'Hotel Bernini Palace? She mentioned she was the new curator, so maybe she was checked into the hotel until she found a permanent place to live. Or maybe this assignment was so sensitive she couldn't afford to be seen talking with an art detective at her office or anywhere in the center city.

"We recently loaned a selection of Botticelli studies of *The Birth of Venus* to the High Museum of Art in Atlanta for an exhibit," the woman said. "The sketch in question was done in preparation for the finished piece, specifically a detail for the face of the model of Venus. You know studies can be traced back to the Italian Renaissance. Art historians even have some of Michelangelo's studies."

"Did the studies arrive damaged?"

"No, the entire exhibit arrived intact, no problems. There was one study we came by recently from an unknown source. It had just surfaced and naturally we snatched it up, but this study, this latest one, is the piece at issue. I got a call about it from the High's curator, one of my college classmates, who told me if this study is real, then the painting in the Uffizi is a fake. A fake! Outrageous, I know. *The Birth of Venus* is one of the most famous and beloved artworks in the world and one of Firenze's top tourist attractions. It is a symbol of Florence itself. People come to the Uffizi specifically for our Botticellis. I asked her if she was sure, and she said, 'Yes.' "

"Isn't it typical for artists to show changes in the light, color, and composition of their work as they gain fresh insights while exploring the subject?" Hadley asked. "Especially if they encounter problems in rendering them?"

"Yes, there have been cases where an artist started out drawing or sketching a man's face and then decided to make the subject a woman," the curator agreed. "Specifically, technological testing revealed some of the revisions Botticelli made on his way to the final artwork."

"I'm familiar," Hadley said. "The Spring goddess to the right of Venus once wore sandals. The hair of Venus, Zephyr to her left, and the goddess in his embrace also underwent transformation. Even the title of the work is not original to the painting. It was added in the nineteenth century. And Botticelli added golden touches after the painting was finished and framed."

"Of course, but that's not what happened here. The layers of the work in the final piece don't reflect the changes in the study," the curator answered.

"Can't you request the study back early so you can do a comparison?"

"That's the problem. If the study in question is real, we'll have our answer. But if it's a fake, what good will it do to compare the two? What if the painting we have at the Uffizi was a reproduction all along? And there's something else. You obviously know your Botticelli."

"He's my favorite artist," Hadley offered.

"Then you know the painting's history," the curator said, biting her lip and scanning the square nervously. "It was believed the painting was ordered as a wedding gift for the cousin of Giuliano Medici and his brother Lorenzo. It hung above the new couple's marriage bed before it was deemed fit to enter the public domain."

Hadley knew that but chose to remain quiet.

"The Uffizi Gallery was established in 1581, commissioned by the patriarch of the de Medicis, Cosimo the First, in 1560," the curator continued. "Anna Maria Louisa, the last Medici heiress, established the museum through a family pact that dictated all of her possessions were never to leave Florence. The Uffizi opened its doors to the public in 1765."

All facts known to any art history major.

"The painting would be impossible to borrow today," the woman chattered in a high-pitched voice. "We'd never take a chance that it could be damaged in transit or stolen. But on January 1, 1930, it was part of one of the most important exhibitions—the Exhibition of Italian Art, 1200-1900, at the Royal Academy in London. Benito Mussolini, the Italian dictator, was listed in the program as an honorary president."

That fascinating fact was one that had escaped Hadley.

"And did you know that in 1938 Benito Mussolini escorted Adolph Hitler for two hours in Florence's Uffizi gallery? Hitler was already planning a colossal art museum in his hometown of Linz, Austria. Three years later, Mussolini had the Uffizi pack up thirty-four crates of art and send them to Germany. Outgoing art continued to flow even after Mussolini was deposed and the Allies headed toward Tuscany."

Hadley did know that the Germans had hidden another cache of paintings in Castello di Montegufoni, a thirteenth-century castle in Florence. There were two hundred and sixty-one works of art stolen from the Uffizi and Palazzo Pitti, another Florence art museum. Among them was Botticelli's *The Birth of Venus*. It was one of the paintings plundered by the Nazis and turned over to The Monuments, Fine Arts, and Archives (MFAA) section of the Allied armies, who returned it to the Uffizi in 1945. So the switch could have been made as early as the Second World War to either the original or the studies.

"Between Hitler and Hermann Göring's systematic looting of Europe's art collections, and the fire-sale of art seized from German citizens before the war and sold at auction, the entire contents of the Uffizi Museum, the museums of Paris, and the treasures of dozens of churches were stripped by the Nazis."

"Yes, I know," said Hadley. "During the Second

World War, the Germans hid tens of thousands of masterpieces in secret underground storage facilities, like salt mines, and in the Italian homes and villas of high-ranking SS officers, for use after the war. There are many pieces still missing. The stolen art trade is a multi-billion-dollar global business, the third largest behind drugs and arms trafficking."

The curator, who hadn't yet introduced herself, relaxed, confident in Hadley's professed knowledge.

"I see you understand. So, our painting has had quite a history."

"Did you notify the Carabinieri Art Squad? Or the superintendent for the arts at the cultural ministry, or at least the local police?"

"No."

"Why not?"

"What if this would get out, that *The Birth of Venus* is possibly a fake? I can't take that chance. I have to verify it another way."

"Could the study be a fake?"

"Not to our knowledge. But it is a possibility. Either the study or the painting hanging in the Uffizi—or both could be imitations."

"Can you have the painting at the Uffizi authenticated?"

"I can't risk it. What if it is a fake? What if the painting returned in the forties was not the real one? How can I explain how that happened?" The curator was adamant. "No one must know about this."

Suddenly, Hadley understood the curator's predicament and why she hadn't called in government officials. She couldn't risk them discovering even the hint that the masterpiece might be a fake. But how to explain the discrepancy between the completed painting and the study that had happened under her watch? So she had called in old reliable Signore Domingo, who had lost most of his important connections in the art world and could be relied upon for secrecy. If he failed in his mission and talked about it, no one would believe him. Did this woman know the Signore was desperate?

"So either the study was switched in transit, stolen and replaced in Atlanta, or the painting that has been hanging on our wall since it was donated by the Medici family was a fake all along, or the painting returned to us by the Monuments Men was a fake. I have to find the original study and get it back before my director or the Advisory Board notices."

"Was the study on canvas?"

"Yes, medium tempera on canvas, just as the master rendered his work in the 1480s, the first artist in Tuscany to do so."

"At six by nine feet, could the painting really be a fake? How would a thief carry it out? Of course, he could strip it from the frame and roll it up, but it's too famous to unload."

"Exactly. It's priceless, but not for sale."

"So our assignment is to track down the original Botticelli study of the face of Venus, if there is one, and return it to you so you can compare it with the original hanging in the Uffizi?"

"Yes, or the original painting itself, if ours is a fake. A tall order, I know. I will pay handsomely." The woman handed Hadley a large manila envelope. "Here's everything you'll need, any information we know about the provenance of the work, and details about the study. Perhaps that will provide some leads. Here's my card, with my cell phone number on the back. Call me any time of the day or night. But this is not to get out to the press, to the public, to the police, to anyone. It would be a scandal that would taint the museum and destroy my career."

"I understand," said Hadley. She took the proffered envelope, put it in her purse, and shook the woman's hand. "You can trust me, er, Signore Domingo. We work as a team."

"Of course, you can charge me for all expenses incurred."

Hadley was more than happy to oblige. Who knew where the hunt would take her? And if she accomplished her mission, this contact at the Uffizi could propel her on her career path.

She watched the "cloak and dagger" curator from the museum walk back in the direction of her hotel. She signaled Luca to come out of hiding.

"Did you get her picture?"

"Yes, I used the telephoto lens. It was dark, but here, you can still see her face."

"Great."

"Why do you need her photo?"

"Rule Number One of Signore Domingo's *Pocket Guide to Art Theft Recovery* is Don't Overlook the Obvious. Better to be safe than sorry. Leave no stone unturned. It's best to be prepared. Any detail, large or small, could be critical."

She explained the situation to her boyfriend.

"What now?" Luca asked.

"I don't know."

"You're the art historian."

"And you're the policeman."

"I have a contact at the art crime department."

Hadley dug her fingers into Luca's arm and whispered furiously. "No police involved, except you. This *has* to stay between us. I've taken the next week off. We have one week to solve this case. What does your schedule look like?"

"I have some vacation time coming. I can take off some days if you need me. But I'll have to ask my sister to watch Bocelli."

"I do need you," Hadley said, wrapping herself against him, laying her lips on Luca's, deepening the kiss.

"You don't have to seduce me, Hadley. I'm at your disposal, always."

"Good to know. Let's continue this conversation back at your place and come up with a plan."

Her suggestive tone implied that *she* was at his disposal as well.

Luca lived in the Ultra Arno, on the other side of the Arno River, connected by the Ponte Vecchio, the bridge that used to be home to fishmongers and butchers and now sparkled with gold and jewelry shops, the only original bridge to survive the Second World War. So they were close to his apartment, and both were anxious to be alone together.

"Hop on," said Luca, revving up his motor and his motorbike. "Bocelli will be happy to see you."

She'd almost forgotten about Bocelli. Luca was crazy about his dog, an adorable Italian Greyhound named after the popular Italian tenor. Luca even sang romantic arias to the sight hound, and Bocelli howled back. The two of them were like Nelson Eddy and Jeanette MacDonald serenading each other in *Indian*

Love Call, a song her grandmother used to sing.

Bocelli was an noble Italian breed that Luca had had since the dog was a pup. Supposedly, the line originated in early Greece and Turkey more than two thousand years ago. They were a favorite breed of Italians during the sixteenth century and coveted by royals as companion dogs. And he was a beautiful dog.

On the minus side, Bocelli had a coat that occasionally shed, and he needed daily exercise. He was speedy, and he loved to run, and he was a great jumper, so Luca had to build a fence around his house to keep Bocelli in. If the dog wasn't chasing rabbits and squirrels, he stuck by Luca's side. On the plus side, he was intelligent and perceptive and sensitive to Luca's voice and his moods. And Luca's voice was amazing. She'd first heard him singing in the shower.

"You have a really good voice. Did you ever think about singing professionally?"

"I've always wanted to be a policeman. My father was a policeman, and so was his father."

"The world is missing out."

She later found out that his coworkers called him "the Voice."

Luca didn't like to be away from Bocelli for very long. She'd have some convincing to do to keep the man and his dog apart for an entire week.

Chapter Three

Before they left on their trip, Hadley insisted they make one stop. She had to view *The Birth of Venus* herself, again. Surely, she could tell if it was a fake. She was no artist or art restorer, but she would know innately if it was a forgery. Botticelli's spark of brilliance could not be replicated or imitated.

She expected the Botticelli Room to be crowded, and it was. She stood in front of the iconic masterpiece to capture that moment in time, cameras clicking, camera sticks waving, people interrupting her view. Every time she saw the painting, and she'd seen it more times than she could count, it spoke to her heart and captured her imagination.

She saw what she always saw in the painting she jokingly called *Venus on the Half Shell*. She could recite from memory the description of the masterpiece after studying it tirelessly in art history class. It portrayed a sensuous, divinely beautiful Venus naked on a seashell floating in to the seashore on gently breaking waves. On her left, the winds Zephyr and Aura gently caressed her with a shower of roses. On her right a handmaid, one of the Three Graces, waited for the goddess to approach so she could cover her nakedness. The meadow was sprinkled with violets. Bright colors, painted with a mixture of egg yolk and light paint, made it look more like a fresco. Some of the details were decorated with traces of gold. The leaves of the orange trees in the background, the ringlets of Venus's hair, and the fluttering cloaks and drapery of the figures were in motion.

No, this was the original. It had to be. She was more convinced than ever. She'd stake her career on it. She *was* staking her career on it. She would have to find the original study to prove that the study at the High Museum was a forgery, which would confirm that the painting at the Uffizi was the real thing.

She wasn't quite sure how to go about it, but she knew she couldn't afford to fail. Too much was at stake—Signore Domingo's reputation and his business, her livelihood.

She hurried to where Luca was waiting on his motorcycle.

"Did you get what you came for?"

"I'm convinced the painting in the Uffizi is real, which means the study is a fake. Now we have to track down the missing Botticelli study."

"What if the painting in the Uffizi *is* a fake?"

"Unlikely, but then we'll have to track down the original."

"Where do we start?"

"I've gone over the history of the painting. There are some gaps in the provenance. We should start there."

Luca drove them back to her apartment. On the way, they passed Florence Cathedral, the Duomo. He took his right hand off the handlebars of the motorbike and squeezed her hands wrapped around his waist. She couldn't hear him over the traffic noise, but she knew what he was thinking. You could get married at the Duomo. There was a long waiting list, but it was possible. He hadn't proposed yet. They had just known each other six months, but she knew that was his wish. It was a romantic thought, but they weren't at that point in their relationship. At least, *she* wasn't ready to commit—to him or anyone. Certainly not to King Charles, or she would have returned home by now.

When they arrived, she retrieved her packed travel bag. Luca's backpack stood erect beside hers like a silent sentry.

Hadley inched toward Luca and patted his thigh.

"Cara Mia, we don't have time for that. We'll miss our train."

Hadley scoffed. "That's not why I was patting you down. Are you carrying a gun?"

"It's a dangerous world, Dolcezza."

"Don't sweetheart me. Are you packing?"

"Bella, I've already packed," said Luca, feigning innocence, pointing to his backpack. "I'm ready to go."

"Luca Ferrari, it is illegal to carry weapons in public places. Answer my question."

"I have a hunting license and a hunting permit."

"It is not hunting season. And we're not going to a game preserve."

"But we are going hunting, are we not?"

"For a painting."

"Art theft is a dangerous game, Fragolina."

"Fragolina?"

"What?"

"You just called me your little strawberry."

"It's a term of endearment."

"For a child. We are equal partners."

"Carabinieri have policing powers that can be exercised at any time and in any part of the country. We are always permitted to carry our assigned weapon as personal equipment. Now, if you would like to check out my personal equipment—"

Hadley opened his jacket and pulled out a Beretta 91FS pistol.

"What is this?"

"Cara Mia, it's loaded," he barked. "Put that back, please."

"What am I going to do with you, Amore Mio?"

"If you don't mind missing our train, I could show you."

Hadley sighed. Sometimes, Luca had a one-track mind. "Never mind. Let's just go."

They arrived at the Florence Santa Maria Novella train station. Luca parked and chained his motorcycle, then went into the station to buy them some bottled water and snacks for the train.

Hadley had already printed out their tickets to Munich.

They waited at the platform for the direct City Night Line Sleeper Train.

When the train arrived, they found their first-class compartment and stored their luggage.

"I never travel first-class," Luca observed.

"The client is paying," Hadley explained. "The train leaves shortly after ten p.m., and we arrive at the München Hauptbahnhof at about six-thirty tomorrow morning. It's the quickest and most convenient route, but we're going to miss out on some stunning scenery."

"Will we be staying overnight in Munich? I hear they have some great beer."

"I'm not planning to. We're just going to cross this one item off the list. Rule it out. We'll be at the state offices when they open, and then we should be on our way, unless we can gain access to Edda Göring's house."

"Edda Göring?"

"Hermann Göring's daughter."

"That monster had a daughter?"

"Yes, a wife and a daughter."

And, according to the curator, a mistress.

Chapter Four

München (Munich), Germany

The following afternoon, Hadley pulled out the curator's business card and tapped into her phone the private number she'd written on the back. The woman answered on the first ring.

"We've hit a dead end in Munich," Hadley reported.

"I was afraid of that," said the curator. "What happened?"

"You know how we assumed Göring had turned some of his looted jewelry, furniture, property, and artwork over to his wife or to his daughter Edda, who lived with him at his country estate, Carinhall."

"Yes."

"When she was baptized, Edda received several works of art as gifts, but she lost them in court battles. Over the years, she petitioned the Bavarian state government to return some of her father's art collection but, ultimately, she was not successful. She did get to keep her jewelry.

"I checked with the state, and to their knowledge, Edda did not have possession of any of her father's artwork when she passed away in Munich in December 2018. She lived alone, so they couldn't confirm if there were any heirs. Did you know Hitler was her godfather?"

"Charming."

"Apparently, she was very proud of her father to the end. And she associated with people of like-minded political views."

"So, what's your next step?"

"We're going to Venice to check on the address you gave me of the woman you think may have been Göring's mistress at one time."

"Perfect. Keep me informed."

"Of course."

"Give my regards to Signore Domingo."

Hadley crossed her fingers behind her back. "I certainly will." She had become a consummate liar.

Hadley had already gone down the list of Signore Domingo's contacts in Venice and, coincidentally, the address the curator had given and the address in the Signore's contact book were the same. So the place or the person on the list was already on the Signore's radar. Had he been to the address before? Met with anyone at the villa? And, if so, what reason did he have to go there?

Hadley had followed Rule Number One in Signore Domingo's *Pocket Guide*—Don't Overlook the Obvious. It made perfect sense, then, that the first, most obvious place to look was at Göring's daughter. But her estate had already been probated and they had come up empty-handed. What they found could have been handled with a phone call, and it had turned out to be a wasted day, but better to be safe than sorry, leave no stone unturned. So it was on to Venice.

Chapter Five

München, Germany to Venezia (Venice), Italy

"We're going to take the ICE—the Intercity-Express—Deutsche Bahn's fastest train."

"First class?"

"Yes," Hadley confirmed. "It's a pretty long train ride."

"Will we stay overnight?"

"Yes, and if we find what we're looking for, maybe several nights."

"On the Grand Canal?"

"Of course. At the Gritti Palace."

"One room or two?"

"One suite," Hadley said. "We have to economize somewhere. And the client doesn't know you're here. Rather, she thinks I'm traveling with Signore Domingo. One suite is cheaper than two rooms. She asked if I minded sharing, and I said no."

"The Gritti Palace is a luxury hotel."

"I'm aware."

"I could get used to being a kept man."

Hadley rolled her eyes.

Luca stored their bags, and Hadley placed her notes on the spacious desk between their seats. There was plenty of legroom. She spread out the files to review before they arrived in Venice. There was a photocopy of the study in question, the face of a model, definitely drawn by Botticelli. It had all his signature style, but it wasn't the face of the goddess in *The Birth of Venus.*

"Why are we going to Venice?" Luca asked.

"Because that's where the trail went cold."

"What trail?"

"We know Hermann Göring, Hitler's second-in-command, had possession of the painting at one time. The German government seized most of Göring's collection. It says in this file folder that the main lodge at Carinhall had a large private art gallery—Göring's own gigantic art museum—where thousands of stolen masterpieces Göring plundered from private collections and museums around Europe since 1939 were showcased.

"He worked hand in hand with an organization whose mission was to loot artwork from Jewish collections, libraries, and museums throughout Europe. Some twenty-six thousand railroad cars full of art treasures and other plundered items were sent to Germany from France. Göring visited Paris repeatedly to select items to be put on a special train to Carinhall and his other homes. His personal collection included thousands of pieces and was valued at two hundred million dollars. The Gestapo were arresting Jewish men all over Germany. Göring amassed a personal fortune by confiscating Jewish property when the victims were deported south—an almost certain death sentence—or forced to vacate their homes and flee the country, liquidating their assets, which included paintings, which were 'bought' at fire-sale prices. The lucky ones managed to escape to Palestine or any country that would take them.

"During World War Two, the Nazis looted six hundred thousand priceless paintings from displaced Jewish victims. But it was never enough. At least a hundred thousand of those pieces are still missing.

"Göring built massive underground bunkers," Hadley continued. "He left Carinhall on April 20, 1945, to make an appearance at Hitler's birthday, and then headed toward Berchtesgaden to attend to 'important tasks' awaiting him in southern Germany.

"Göring knew the Reich was imploding," Hadley reported. "Before he left Carinhall, he gave a small unit of Luftwaffe soldiers the orders to blow up the estate as soon as the Red Army was in sight. The Soviets advanced on Carinhall on April 28, 1945—and the soldiers did their job blowing up Carinhall with the aid of more than eighty aircraft bombs."

"Wouldn't he have left the valuables to his wife or daughter?" Luca wondered.

"That would have been too obvious. And we verified that wasn't the case in Munich."

"Then why Venice?"

"While Göring was in Salzburg, the curator thinks he slipped away to Venice to deliver some paintings to his former mistress for safekeeping."

"How can we find her?"

"The curator provided an address. Her name was Karrissa Montanari. She wouldn't be alive today. We'll have to see if she has any surviving relatives."

Chapter Six

Venezia, Italy

Luca helped Hadley down from the train, then went back to retrieve their luggage.

The Venezia Santa Lucia Railway Station was packed. Luca led the way to the Ferrovia vaporetto landing stage immediately in front of the station on the banks of the Grand Canal and hailed a water taxi that would take them to the private pier of the iconic Grand Canal luxury hotel, the Gritti Palace. She was looking forward to staying at the fifteenth-century palazzo that had housed noble families and famous visitors since 1895. She had been to Venice before but never with Luca, and they were excited at the prospect of enjoying the city together as tourists while conducting their business.

Hadley savored the inspiring vistas of Venice as the water taxi traveled directly under the Rialto bridge. The sun-dappled deep blue-green water rippled in rich contrast to pale yellow of the Ca' d'Oro, the golden house—in her opinion, the jewel of the Grand Canal. She took out her cell phone and snapped a picture of Luca in profile with the Palazzo Santa Sofia in the background.

Hadley's command of the Italian language was crude, at best. Luca teased that she sounded like a child when speaking it, although he found it endearing, so she had no problem letting him take the lead with the desk clerk when they checked into the hotel.

Hadley couldn't believe the luxurious room—the antiques, the Murano glass, the original artwork on the walls, and the magnificent view of Santa Maria delle Salute church on the Grand Canal. The bathroom was like something from an architectural magazine. She had never seen anything like it. They were, at most, a five-minute walk from La Fenice Opera House, which was across the street from the restaurant where they had reservations later that evening. The convenient vaporetto water bus stop at Santa Maria del Giglio offered inexpensive transportation anywhere in the city.

She wanted to explore La Serenissima—take a gondola down the lagoons of the city of love, visit the churches, which housed beautiful art, and, of course, the museums, the Peggy Guggenheim Collection (although her taste didn't particularly run to modern), the Galleria dell'Accademia and the Doge's Palace. And the food, well, it was a given that they'd sample all the culinary delights of Venice and people-watch at Piazza San Marco.

On Hadley's first trip to Venice she had eaten a plateful of calamari fritti before she knew she was eating fried squid. Now, that was her favorite appetizer. But first, Luca was on the menu. They would eat after christening the king-size bed in their suite, which they proceeded to do.

In the end, they missed their dinner reservation. They were so tired from the long train ride they didn't get up until ten the next morning.

"I'm hungry," said Luca, his stomach growling, studying the hotel guide. "Why don't we have breakfast at the Gritti Terrace waterfront?"

"You're always hungry. We overslept. Table service would take too long. We can grab something on the way to our destination."

Frowning, Luca showed the concierge the address, and the man at the desk pointed the way in Italian with all the accompanying expressive hand signals.

"It's only a few minutes away," Luca announced.

"Probably why the curator suggested this hotel," Hadley replied.

"One night here cost about one week's pay," Luca said. "You have expensive tastes, Cara."

"*Good* taste," Hadley corrected. "I chose you, didn't I?"

"Vero. But still you are, how do you say in America, high maintenance?"

Hadley laughed but didn't deny it. She appreciated beautiful things, and she slowed her pace to study Luca's backside, which she likened to a masterpiece.

Chapter Seven

After enjoying a light breakfast on the go and stopping along the way to look in the window of the galleries, at Hadley's insistence, they arrived at the address the curator had provided.

"Nice house," Luca observed. "Right on the Grand Canal. It's as big as a palace."

"It's a villa," Hadley said. "Villa Montanari. Let's see if anyone's at home."

Hadley rang the doorbell.

She heard some footsteps on the other side of the door. The door opened and a beautiful young lady stood before them. She was perhaps in her early thirties, with long blonde hair, blue eyes the color of the Mediterranean Sea, and a big smile.

Hadley offered her hand. "Hello, I'm Hadley Evans, and this is Luca Ferrari."

"Can I help you?"

"We're looking for the residence of Karrissa Montanari."

"She was my grandmother. She passed away many years ago. My mother, Serena Spinelli, is also gone. There are just the two of us now—my brother Matteo and me. I'm Isabella."

"Could we come in and talk to you?" Hadley asked.

"May I ask what this is about?"

"I've…we've…come about the painting."

Isabella's mouth opened in surprise. She clutched her hands. The welcoming smile disappeared from her face, and she was visibly shaking.

"The painting? My b-brother is not at home, but I'm expecting him soon. You cannot be here."

"Why not?" Hadley asked, puzzled.

"Because—" She faltered, and then she lapsed into a string of Italian.

At a loss, Hadley looked at Luca for a translation.

"She says her brother would not like us to be here."

Isabella's face lost its color. She looked like she was about to faint, and when she did, Luca caught her up in his strong arms and carried her into the house, depositing her gently on an oversized couch.

"Hadley, she's scared to death of something. Of her brother, I think."

Hadley closed the door behind them.

Luca sat down beside the girl and took her hand. "Isabella, wake up, please," he whispered in earnest.

Luca seemed in a trance, intent on reenacting a scene from *Sleeping Beauty*. He fanned Isabella's pale face with a magazine he found on the end table and looked as if he might kiss her.

"Luca, for heaven's sake, snap out of it," Hadley scolded, thinking, the girl was stunning, no doubt about it—stunning enough to be a model—a painter's model—or a movie star—but Luca had morphed into a knight in shining armor, a lap dog, eager to come to the rescue of the beautiful maiden. She needed to check her insecurities at the door. Wasn't that one of the things she loved about him? Hadley walked into the spacious, chef-worthy kitchen with a view to die for, and wet her hands under the sink. She walked back to the living room and sprinkled a few drops on Isabella's face. The girl gradually opened her eyes.

"Isabella!" Luca exclaimed. "You're awake."

Hadley rolled her eyes.

Isabella sat up, an anxious look on her face. "Matteo could be here any minute. You need to leave now."

"What are you afraid of?" Luca asked.

"Matteo is very protective. He doesn't tolerate strangers."

Hadley sensed the girl's fear. It coated the room like a fog. Was there an unnatural relationship between brother and sister?

"He is your brother," Luca reasoned. "Surely, you're not afraid of your own brother."

"My twin," Isabella confirmed. "Matteo has what you call a hot head."

Hadley laughed. "You mean your brother is a hothead."

"He can be disagreeable…and quite dangerous when the mood hits him. He's very—strict."

"I won't let anything happen to you," Luca vowed.

Hadley shook her head. Luca seemed smitten. "Should I leave you two alone?"

"Can't you see she's terrified?" Luca whispered, still holding Isabella's hand in his.

"Of her own brother?"

Hadley took the opportunity to press their case.

"Isabella, we're not here to harm you. I'm from the Massimo Domingo Art Detective Agency in Florence. We're trying to track down a Botticelli study, a sketch. Do you know anything about that?"

After a brief period of silence, she spoke.

"I've been waiting for you for many years."

"What do you mean?"

"Come, but we must be quick." She rose carefully from the couch, and they followed her upstairs down a long hallway to the last door on the right. She took a key from around her neck and unlocked the door. The room was dark, but when Isabella turned on the ceiling-mounted accent lights, Hadley fought to breathe.

"Oh, my," she whispered. "It can't be. My God, Luca." Hadley felt lightheaded. She hadn't eaten enough for breakfast. She began to lose consciousness. But she was not going to faint like that frail beauty Isabella or melt into a pool of helplessness… When she came to, she was lying in Luca's arms.

He had carried her over to a wide velvet-lined bench in the middle of the room, a round room, a large room. Either the room was spinning or her head was spinning. And on the wall, on the stark white wall, right in front of her eyes, hung an ornately framed, breathtaking Botticelli. Not *The Birth of Venus*, not *Primavera,* but the rendition of another goddess on another life-size canvas. A medium tempera on canvas, with bright colors and traces of gold in the hair of the mythical, barely clothed Goddess Diana, twin sister of Apollo. The virgin goddess of childbirth and chastity, shrouded by moonlight in a tranquil woodland scene depicting wild animals and the hunt, surrounded by her sacred cypress trees, undisturbed by a lover. The face of the model in the study sent to The High Museum of Art in Atlanta.

It couldn't be. Hadley got up slowly from the couch and walked up to the painting. It wasn't signed. Of course, it wasn't. Botticelli didn't sign his paintings. The only piece he ever signed was *Mystic Nativity*, his last major work.

This painting, this masterpiece, was reminiscent of his most famous complementary paintings in the Uffizi gallery. But once Botticelli had fallen under the influence of the puritan fanatic friar, the Italian Christian preacher Girolamo Savonarola, moral dictator of Florence, his later works were religious in keeping with his newfound piety, not secular like this painting. Although Hadley still preferred his earlier works, she found beauty in the splendid symbolic imagery of his later paintings. Religious or secular, she would recognize his signature style anywhere.

"W-what is this?" she asked Isabella.

"*Amore*," Isabella answered simply.

"But how…where did this come from? H-how did you get it?"

If paintings could talk, what secrets would this masterpiece reveal?

Isabella expelled a breath. "It is a long story. A story that overlaps my family history."

"I need to hear it. I need to know all about this painting. Is it genuine?" If so, the value of the painting would be inestimable—at a minimum in the hundreds of millions of dollars.

"I am sure of it. Just like the rest."

"The rest?"

"Look around," Isabella said, indicating the circular space.

Hadley had been too intensely focused on the Botticelli in front of her to notice the rest of the room. When she turned in place, she saw them, other, smaller yet no less precious, paintings by Botticelli and others. Were they all plundered by the Nazis? Hard to classify them as missing when no one knew of their existence.

Typically, a painting would turn up after the thief attempted to sell it. But these gems had been hidden in a private home, this private home, for more than seventy-five years—by Göring—a notorious art hoarder. He and Hitler were in a perpetual race to collect—aka steal—works of art. Were they stolen from an art dealer? From a collection? Then why hadn't they ever been reported missing?

"But these, how can they be here? I've never seen some of these before or read anything about them." It was believed that the *Primavera* and *The Birth of Venus* were a part of a much grander series that Botticelli was planning. This theory had fallen out of favor with the majority of art historians, but if it were true, *Amore* would be his third. The puzzle pieces were beginning to fall into place.

The historical record of whether Sandro Botticelli had burned several of his paintings based on classical mythology in the Florentine bonfire of 1497 was unclear. Could these be some thought to be destroyed in the bonfire of the vanities, where thousands of precious artworks were set on fire in the name of artistic excesses? Could Botticelli have had second thoughts about burning his remaining pagan works in the midst of his religious crisis and held back these paintings from the world? Somehow, if they were authentic, they had gotten into the hands of a private art patron, the Medicis perhaps, the Vatican, the Sforzas—the ruling family of Milan—and ended their circuitous journey in this Venetian villa. A Titian, the greatest Italian Renaissance painter of the Venetian school, would be a more likely find in this city, but this painting...these paintings...were incongruent but no less priceless. If that scenario were true, this would be the greatest art discovery in history.

Chapter Eight

"Hermann Göring, my grandfather, was madly in love with his first wife Carin, but when she died in 1931, he was desperately lonely, and on a trip to Venice, he met my grandmother, Karrissa. They were together on and off until 1935, when he married Emmy Sonnemann, a beautiful German actress from Hamburg, with a gala reception at the Berlin Opera House. Hitler was his best man. Their daughter, Edda, was born three years later.

"By then, he had all but forgotten Karrissa. Occasionally, he would appear out of the blue with another painting to hide, and she would allow him back into her bed. What choice did she have? He was one of the most powerful men in Europe. Not all of the paintings are on display in this room. There are many crates of his in the villa, on the upper level, including studies of *Amore* by Botticelli."

Isabella walked over to a marble table and lifted two framed photographs and brought them over to Hadley and Luca.

"This is my grandmother with Göring."

"She's beautiful," Hadley said. "She is the image of you."

"Everyone says so." She held up the second photograph.

"This is a picture of Matteo and me." The picture showed a young man next to an adolescent girl, his arm slung possessively around her shoulder. Evil seemed to emanate from his eyes. He was the image of his grandfather, Hermann Göring.

"This is where our story begins. Herr Göring visited often. My grandmother was very young and innocent. She was only twenty, and he was forty-one, but no matter, just like Mussolini was twenty-eight years older than his mistress. Grandfather pursued Karrissa, showered her with gifts, made pretty promises he never kept. She relished the attention of the prominent, older man, one of the richest, most powerful men on the continent. She was in love with him. She provided comfort to him after the death of his beloved wife, Carin. But in the end, his attentions were focused on Emmy Sonnemann. She was sophisticated and available, in Berlin, whereas my unworldly grandmother was out of sight and out of mind in Venice.

"My grandmother could feel her hold on the Luftwaffe Commander-in-Chief slipping. Pictures of Emmy and Hermann were in all the newspapers. She often served as Hitler's hostess at state events. After they married in 1935, she was 'First Lady of the Third Reich,' freezing out even Hitler's future wife, Eva Braun. I don't think Emmy ever knew about Karrissa.

"When my grandmother found herself pregnant as a result of one of his secret visits in 1938, Hermann installed her in this villa. Göring owned many mansions, estates, and castles, so purchasing another villa didn't raise any eyebrows. This Venetian villa belonged to a wealthy Jewish family in Berlin eager to escape to America, and he got it for a fraction of its worth, along with all of its contents, which included some of the artwork you see on the walls today and in the rest of the house. He set my grandmother up in their love nest, continued to support her and their illegitimate daughter, and built this room for the paintings he hid here. But when Emmy and Hermann's daughter Edda was born, he stopped coming around."

"What about the family who owned this home? Did they ever make it to America?"

"All that I know is documented in my grandmother's diary. Many of them remained trapped in Europe and were sent to the death camps. No one came back to claim this house after the war."

"What happened to Emmy?"

"Oh, it's not really my family's history, but I've always been interested in the story. So I did some research and found that she was sent to jail for a year after the end of the war, and thirty percent of her property was confiscated. She died in Munich in 1973 at the age of 80. But no one confiscated our villa because no one knew about it.

"After the Soviets approached Berlin, Hitler admitted defeat and made plans to remain in Berlin and commit suicide. Then Carinhall was evacuated and destroyed. A large part of Göring's private collection had already been moved to a converted salt mine in Altausee, Austria. In January 1945, he moved most of his remaining art to the tunnels of Berchtesgaden and other locations.

"He made the final trip to Venice to hide some of the more priceless pieces and install them in the museum he'd built in our villa. This is what you see here. Then he rushed back to his estate in Obersalzburg in April 1945. He and my grandmother never saw each other again.

"The Americans found parts of Göring's art

collection when they captured him on May 7, 1945, in Schloss Fischhorn in Salzburger Pinzgau.

"He was a coward, my grandfather," Isabella said icily. "He swallowed a cyanide pill and committed suicide, like Hitler, in his prison cell, rather than face up to his crimes, the night he was condemned to hang as a convicted war criminal. I am so ashamed of my grandfather, my heritage.

"I don't blame my grandmother," she added. "Göring wasn't responsible for the 'total solution' of the 'Jewish question,' or at least not until 1938. By then Karrissa was in too deep, and she had already given birth to my mother."

"Do you have any documentation of this story?" Hadley asked.

"Besides the paintings, only my grandmother's diary and the Botticelli studies of *Amore*," Isabella said. "It's all there, our dirty family history. My grandmother said someone would come one day, and we were to turn over the contents of the museum and the crates. I assumed it would be his wife, Emmy, or his daughter, but they are both dead. I've been waiting. And now you have come.

"I know Matteo has been selling off some of the works through third parties, to support us," Isabella stated. "We were warned not to do that. He sold one of the studies of *Amore* to the Uffizi Gallery. He was planning to sell *Amore* to the highest bidder, a wealthy private art collector. He doesn't appreciate the art, just the profit. The people he deals with are not very nice. They scare me. When I pleaded with him not to sell, he slapped me and threatened me. No one outside the family has ever seen this museum."

She paused. "Do you believe someone can be born evil, Signorina Evans?"

Hadley shrugged.

"My brother is evil," Isabella whispered, trembling. "I myself have decided not to marry and have children because I don't want to take a chance of bringing another evil person into this world. Matteo wouldn't allow it anyway. He is very controlling. I am his—" Isabella broke into tears. "I am…so ashamed."

Hadley could not be sure, but from the way Isabella was talking, it sounded like her brother was abusing her.

Luca balled one of his hands into a fist and punched the other hand, eager to take on Matteo, a monster he had yet to meet.

Hadley thought it was a shame such a beautiful girl would deny herself love and happiness and children because of an accident of birth. Was that what she was doing by denying a more serious relationship with Luca? Was she going to return to America to marry King Charles when all she wanted and needed was right here in front of her?

Isabella went to a drawer in the beautiful antique desk near the door and returned to hand Hadley her grandmother's diary.

"I don't know when he will do it, but I am sure he will try to sell *Amore*. I've heard him on the telephone. He's been enticing dealers with the studies, introducing them, in an attempt to drive up the price. If he finds you here, he will kill you. If he discovers I've told you, he will not hesitate to kill me, too.

"It's past time," Isabella continued. "I want the world to know, to see these beautiful pictures. No one else is coming. Will you help me?"

"Yes," Hadley assured her.

"Now you must go. Matteo cannot find you here. Come back in the morning when he is gone off to whatever it is he does all day."

Luca hesitated. Hadley pulled out her cell phone to call the curator. She rifled through her handbag but couldn't find the woman's business card. So she called the Uffizi.

"Could you please connect me to the museum curator?"

"Signore Caruso is not in his office."

"No, this is a woman, the new curator to the gallery."

"There is only one curator. Signore Caruso."

"She's new. She may not have started yet."

"There's been a hiring freeze for months. There are no new female employees."

Hadley frowned. "Sorry to have bothered you."

Why would that woman lie to her? She finally located the business card. But there was no name on the front of the card, only a number scribbled hastily on the back. Hadley dialed the number.

The mystery woman answered right away.

"Where are you?" she asked.

"*Who* are *you*?" Hadley challenged.

"What do you mean?"

"I just called the Uffizi, and they've never heard of you."

"That's because I haven't started work yet."

"The woman on the phone doesn't know anything about you."

"The current curator hasn't told them he is resigning. It's all very hush-hush."

Hadley paused. She was in over her head. "I'm in Venice."

"Have you found anything?" Excitement fairly crackled over the telephone lines.

"Yes. Meet us at the villa tomorrow morning." She gave her the address. "Come quickly. And bring boxes and crates, lots of crates."

A feeling of unease crept over Hadley, as she recalled Rule Number Two of the *Pocket Guide*. Watch Your Back. Stolen Art Is A Dangerous Game. Don't Underestimate Your Adversaries. There Are People Who Will Want What You Have And Do Anything To Get It.

"I must alert Signore Domingo," she announced.

Luca placed a reassuring hand over hers. "Cara, this is your case. You deserve all of the credit. You did all the work. You can handle it yourself. I have complete confidence in you. Have you heard of the Reggimento corazzieri?"

"The honor guard of the president of the Italian Republic?"

"Si. Their motto is '*Virtus in periculis firmior*,' which means 'Courage becomes stronger in danger.' "

Luca was trying to make her feel safe. But she was not courageous. And she smelled danger wherever she turned. The villa reeked of it.

Chapter Nine

"I hate to leave Isabella alone tonight," whispered Luca. "She is afraid for her life. I could arrest her brother."

"For what? For thinking of selling a stolen painting that we don't know for sure is stolen or authentic? We should wait for the authorities."

"I *am* the authorities."

"But all we have to go on is hearsay."

"And the diary," Luca reminded her. "You saw the girl. Her brother has all but locked her away in this palace. She is virtually his prisoner. She didn't come out and say it, but I feel sure something is not right with that relationship. I'm not comfortable leaving her."

"But if we take her with us, her brother will suspect something is wrong. He might run off with the painting, or burn it—or worse."

"So you are willing to sacrifice an innocent girl's safety for your precious artwork? Art is all you think about. Your art is more important to you than me."

"That's not true," argued Hadley. "It will take them months to catalog and authenticate all these paintings. But I know they are real. Hidden away in this private villa all these years. We can't afford to lose *Amore*. Luca, can you occupy Isabella for a few minutes while I go back and check something in the gallery? Turn on your charm."

"You expect me to seduce this girl?"

"Do whatever you have to do," Hadley stated flatly, hiding her Furla bag under a decorative pillow on the couch.

Luca stalked off to do his duty, accompanied by Hadley.

"Isabella," Hadley said. "I think I forgot my handbag. Could you let me back into the museum?"

"I don't think…there's not much time before…"

"Isabella," Luca said, placing a calming hand around Isabella's shoulder and rubbing her arm. "Let us take a quick stroll around the villa. Perhaps there's a garden? I think you need some fresh air. Your face is frighteningly pale. Give my colleague the key, and she will retrieve her handbag."

"But I—"

"Hush," Luca whispered, leaning close in to the signorina. "Everything will be all right. Do you trust me?"

Luca placed a featherlight kiss on Isabella's cheek, and she looked adoringly into his eyes.

"If you're sure."

"I'm sure," Luca said.

Disarmed, Isabella removed the lanyard with the key from around her neck and handed it to Hadley.

"Thank you. I'll be right back."

Luca led Isabella out into a glass-enclosed garden.

Don't you dare kiss her again, you snake in the garden.

Hadley suddenly remembered Rule Number Three of Signore Domingo's "Pocket Guide to Stolen Art Recovery." Always Look Beneath the Surface. There's More Than Meets The Eye. You May Be Surprised At

What You Find.

She'd seen a rather large but forgettable painting on the wall opposite *Amore*. It was a hunting scene, perhaps painted by a Dutch Master.

She'd need Luca's help to remove the painting from the wall, to check beneath the paper, to see if, perhaps there was another painting hidden there. Another priceless, undiscovered Botticelli, perhaps? She couldn't do it alone, and she could hardly take the giant painting with her. But she'd bet her career there was a treasure either painted on the back of the canvas or nestled between the nondescript piece of art and its hand-carved frame. That painting was a black swan among white beauties. A definite red flag.

She took a quick look around and snapped some photos of *Amore* and some of the other works of art with her cell phone. She'd have to wait until they returned tomorrow to see if there was a treasure behind the painting opposite *Amore.*

When she locked the museum door and found her way into the garden, Luca's body was wound around Isabella's, and his lips were hungrily devouring hers. Her arms were around his neck and her substantial breasts were pressed against his chest.

"Luca Ferrari!" Hadley cried out.

Luca broke apart from the signorina and had the decency to look guilty.

Isabella's hair was mussed and her lipstick was all over Luca's face, outlining the trace of her kisses. Her chest was heaving, and she looked as if she were going to faint, again. It was obvious to Hadley that the girl was starved for real affection, had never been kissed like that, and was begging for it to happen again. Gritting her teeth, she tried to maintain a semblance of calm.

Hadley pressed the key firmly into Isabella's hand, when what she really wanted to do was scratch the girl's eyes out.

"We will be back in the morning," she said in the calmest voice she could manage.

Isabella, still breathless, nodded, but she was so overcome with lust, she couldn't form any words.

Hadley grabbed Luca's hand and pulled him out the door, almost dislocating his shoulder. When they stood outside, she turned to face him, hands on hips, in her best battle stance.

"What the hell was that all about?"

Luca flashed a devilish smile. "You told me to turn on the charm."

"I didn't tell you to turn on *the girl*. You had your tongue halfway down her throat. If I had come in a moment later, who knows what I would have walked in on?"

"For the record, she had *her* tongue down *my* throat. I was just playing along. Just following orders. A performance." Luca's dimples were showing.

"This ends now, Romeo," Hadley fumed. "And don't even think of getting into my bed tonight. You can sleep on the couch—after you take a cold shower. Or better yet, stay here with your precious Isabella. I don't even want to look at you."

"But, Cara—"

"Don't Cara me. You are such an…Italian. It is never going to work out between us."

"Mi piaci molto."

"You really like me?" Hadley screeched. "Until the next girl comes along. Words, just words. I thought I could count on you."

Were all Italian men like Signore Domingo? Was cheating on their wives second nature to men like that, or a national pastime? She and Luca weren't exactly married, but they were in a committed relationship. Or so she had thought. That must count for something.

"Do you want me to tell you I love you?"

"Not if you have to ask me."

"You're jealous."

"Don't you dare try to define me. Just how far were you going to go?"

"As far as the situation demanded. For you."

"You obviously got carried away. She's inexperienced. You will break her heart." *And mine*.

Outraged, Hadley reached her arm back and took a swing at Luca. He blocked her in mid-swing.

"Remember, I'm armed, Cara."

"I hate you, you…Casanova," Hadley screamed. Her heart beat out of her chest. Steam shot out of her head—or it might have been the settling fog.

Signore Domingo was right. She would heed his rules. *Don't overlook the obvious*. She and Luca were from two different worlds. And, *Always look beneath the surface*—beneath the devoted exterior to find the rotten core.

Hadley rushed off toward the hotel to get as far away from Luca as possible.

****

Hadley stepped off the hotel elevator and used the card key to get into the room. When she was inside, she slammed the door and locked it. Let Luca try to get in. Ha.

She grabbed a polished apple from the fruit basket

on the table and took a bite. Which just reminded her of Isabella and the garden and Luca, the serpent that had enticed the unsuspecting Eve, in the person of Isabella, to do evil. She threw the discarded apple into a waste basket. Then she got into bed, pulled up the covers, and started reading the diary of Karrissa Montanari.

Chapter Ten

Information From Karrissa Montanari's Diary, Venice, Italy, 1934-1946

I met Hermann Göring at a dinner party one night after the opera. I knew he was dangerous the moment we were introduced. I detected the hunger in his eyes, and he detected the vulnerability in mine. But I was ready for some danger. He was a dashing aviator—a fighter pilot ace—a World War I hero, and so handsome in his uniform. A member of the Nazi party, years before Mussolini allied with Germany and the German occupation. He had a lot to recommend him.

Hermann was lonely after the death of his wife, and he pursued me. He knew what he wanted, and he wanted me. I was flattered by his attention and the gifts he lavished on me. I was inexperienced, but he taught me everything I needed to know to satisfy his amorous appetites.

It was rumored he was addicted to morphine, but that was because he had gotten a bullet in his leg and it was the only thing that eased his pain. By then I had fallen hopelessly in love and had become addicted to him. He called me at least five times a day when we weren't together. After Hitler became chancellor of Germany, he appointed Hermann his cabinet minister, so he was busy working hard for the Nazi party and overseeing the creation of the Gestapo. Hermann was the second most powerful man in Germany. Promoted to commander-in-chief of the Luftwaffe the year after we met. People thought of him as ruthless, one of the most sinister and dangerous men in the world, and he suffered mood swings, but in private, he was gentle and sweet. He seemed to genuinely care.

Hermann was often derided for being overweight. But that didn't bother me. He knew he could relax and be himself with me. He confided in me. I was the keeper of his secrets. And when *Amore* surfaced, I was not to whisper a word about it lest Hitler get wind of the masterpiece and demand it for his own private collection.

In the beginning, when our love for each other was new, he made many trips back to Venice so we could be together. I wanted to go slow. It was Hermann who wanted to speed things up. I soon discovered his real mission in the city was to amass a fortune in stolen art. No matter how many paintings he seized, it was never enough.

To Hitler and Göring, artistic plunder was a matter of state policy. The two were in a race to steal artworks. It was as if they were Adoph and Hermann, young boys playing pirate, not grown men. They pilfered the entire contents of the Uffizi Museum, tens of thousands of masterpieces looted from the museums of Paris and occupied Europe, and struck gold by looting religious paintings and sculptures in dozens of churches in countries throughout German-occupied Europe.

Amore captured Hermann's fancy. It was an obsession, really. Not to be outdone by the Führer, Göring scored the Botticelli, the most valuable art treasure the world had *never* known. He learned of the rare painting by Sandro Botticelli from a Swiss art dealer and acquired it (only later did I learn that "acquire" was another name for loot) from a wealthy and prominent Jewish banking family from Berlin that was interested in emigrating to the United States. They "sold" Hermann their Venetian villa, along with *Amore* and more than 500 pieces of art at the family's Venetian vacation home and their main residence in Berlin, in exchange for passage out of Berlin.

I later learned that the banker never made it out of Germany. He was lost in the Holocaust, as were his priceless artifacts. The banker's wife and young son managed to flee the Nazis, but the family's assets—paintings, along with their properties—were appropriated, assets that rightly belonged to the branch of the family that managed to make it to the United States.

After the war, a train car filled with Hermann Göring's stolen art was pillaged by the locals in the Bavarian Alps. But Hermann's most prized paintings stayed safe in our villa in Venice.

By then, Hermann had already started seeing that actress from Hamburg. But that didn't stop him from his regular visits. He set me up in a villa and paid all my expenses. He married Emmy, and they had a daughter together. When I told Hermann I was pregnant, he said he would continue to support me and my daughter. He brought crates of looted art to store at the villa and built the circular gallery room—temperature controlled to protect the paintings.

He said he or someone would be back to collect it, and I was not to sell it off under any circumstances. After the war, after Hermann died, I was constantly expecting a knock on the door, someone saying, "Get out of my house. Return my stolen paintings." But that knock never came. And in time I began to think of the house as mine. But the paintings were sacrosanct. I would never sell them.

The deportations of Italian Jews to Nazi death camps didn't begin until September 1943 when German troops invaded Italy from the north and the Italians surrendered. By that time Hermann and I were not together except for the times he dropped in to add a painting or two to the collection here. In October 1943, Nazis raided the Jewish ghetto in Rome. In November 1943, the Jews of Florence were deported to Auschwitz. About 1,200 Jews were living in Venice when German troops occupied the city in 1943. When the head of the Jewish community in Venice was asked for a list of all the Jews living in Venice, rather than turn it in, he burned every list and took his own life.

Because of his sacrifice, the Nazis were never able to locate the Venetian Jews, and only 243 were deported to concentration camps, including the chief rabbi. Of those 243 who were taken to Auschwitz, only eight returned home. Meanwhile, the rest of the community managed to escape. An estimated 10,000 Italian Jews were deported to concentration camps—7,700 of them perished in the Holocaust.

I remember once at a dinner party, in 1935 I think it was, Hermann saying, "I should not like to be a Jew in Germany." At the time, I didn't know how big a role he played in finding a solution to the "Jewish question." I was blinded by my feelings for him, so blinded I ignored the signs that I was in love with a monster.

Works of art were taken from museums, churches,

individual homes, particularly Jewish collections. Many artworks were never claimed after the war mainly because the individual owner had gone up in smoke in the Holocaust. I was complicit in the scheme without even realizing it.

My daughter Serena married an abusive man, a man who cheated on her. When she left him, she brought the twins to live with me in the villa. We lived a solitary life. We didn't allow people into our home for fear they would discover the paintings in the locked room. We all knew we were to protect the paintings with our lives and were not to share the secret of the hidden museum. Isabella, the angel, was my favorite. Matteo was the image of Hermann in more than looks. He was my flesh and blood, but there was an air of evil about him that was frightening.

Matteo mistakenly believed the paintings were his legacy, much as I tried to correct his notion. They did not belong to our family. We were merely caretakers. One day, I told them, someone would come for them.

****

The diary documented the systematic Nazi thefts and seizures from German citizens of Jewish descent, even before the war, to fund the German war effort. In many cases, Göring's art advisor made the connections and the sale through galleries in Switzerland—also listed in the pages of the diary, so the Reichsmarschall's hands remained clean. Hitler followed suit, ordering the theft of such treasures as the *Mona Lisa* for his super museum in his hometown of Linz. It turned out the *Mona Lisa* Hitler stole was a copy. Perhaps, then, so was the Botticelli in the Uffizi.

Before war erupted in 1939, artworks in the Louvre

were crated and shuttled to villas and castles all over France. Today, Paris's Louvre has more than 1,000 unclaimed works.

The *Mona Lisa* was sent to a castle in the Loire Valley and moved twice in 1940 and a final time in 1942. The real masterpiece was returned to the museum on June 16, 1945.

The Monuments Men found a sixteenth-century copy of daVinci's painting still in the Louvre's possession. The painting that made its way around France was that copy, captured in 1942 by Germans. Meanwhile the real daVinci remained in Paris, hidden in an undisclosed location by the Monuments Men.

Artwork was hidden in underground storage facilities like salt and copper mines, Italian homes, and in the villas of high-ranking SS officers, such as the villa in which Göring had installed his mistress.

I knew that during the war, to avoid being stolen or damaged, paintings such as the masterpieces *Primavera* and *The Birth of Venus* were hidden in Castello di Montegufoni and scattered in many other places throughout the Tuscan countryside. In late July 1944, the allies arrived on the southern bank of the Arno River. The next month, the Nazis grabbed a cache of paintings taken from the Uffizi and hidden in Northern Italy. Another cache of paintings—some 1,261 works of art stolen from the Uffizi and Palazzo Pitti, another Florence art museum, was discovered.

Chapter Eleven

There was a pounding on the door of the hotel suite.
Hadley slipped the diary back into her handbag.

"Open up, Hadley." It was Luca.

She didn't answer, hoping he'd go away.

"Come on," he pleaded. "Don't leave me standing
out here." Luca was normally an even-tempered man, but
when he thought he was in the right, he was like a caged
tiger. It was better not to press him.

She knew he could get into the room. She'd
forgotten to bolt the door. Luca was a police officer, after
all. But she was still angry and hurt.

She recalled Rule Number Four of the *Pocket
Guide*: Don't Waste Time With Distractions. Focus On
The Matter At Hand.

Luca was a classic example of a distraction. He was
handsome, idealistic, principled, caring, demonstrative
(case in point: tongue down the throat of a girl he'd just
met), generous, and above all, loyal, committed, and
responsible. While she was intense, temperamental, and
suspicious. And don't forget *secretive*. King Charles
knew nothing about Luca, and Luca wasn't aware she
had a serious boyfriend waiting for her back home. And
her boss, Massimo Domingo, didn't know she was in
Venice, working for a client behind his back and that she
had borrowed his contact book without permission.

"Go away. Why don't you go back and comfort

Isabella?"

"Do you really want me to do that? Matteo will be back at the villa by now. We can't just barge in. We have to come up with a plan."

Luca was probably right. Rule Number Five of the Guide was Formulate A Plan.

"Then get another room."

"Hadley, you know I can't afford a room at this hotel, at these prices."

"Then sleep outside the door."

"Hadley, you asked me for my help."

Hadley pouted. Did pouts count if the person you were trying to impress wasn't in the room with you?

Resigned, Hadley got up from the bed and opened the door.

"Okay, you can sleep on the couch, but don't dare come anywhere near me. I'm not in the mood for your games tonight."

Luca walked in, removed his gun, and laid it on the end table. He stretched out on the couch, but his body was too big for the sofa. He tossed and turned all night.

The next morning, when she awoke, he was gone. And, now that her emotions had somewhat cooled, she hoped Luca would be waiting for her at the villa. She had missed him in her bed last night, but she had no one to blame but herself. Luca was just being Luca. He was proud, just like any other man.

She'd placed a frantic call to Gerda after she'd decided she really did need Massimo's help. He could be on a train and in Venice in a couple of hours or a little more than two hours by car. But the temp told her Gerda was at the doctor. Again? Was something wrong with Gerda?

She'd ordered room service for them the previous day, knowing they would want an early start, but since Luca had disappeared, she felt obliged to eat his crispy bacon slices and part of his cheese omelet to complement her Belgian waffles. And pick at his fruit cup. After which she dipped the end of his croissant into a mini jar of honey. Then she wrapped the remainder of the croissant in a monogrammed napkin and placed it in her handbag. Before she showered, dressed, and walked toward Isabella's villa, she put in another call to Gerda.

Chapter Twelve

"Massimo Domingo Art Detective Agency."

"Gerda, it's Hadley." She exhaled, relieved to hear her friend's voice. Gerda was a very private person. She would have to approach any questions about health issues with caution.

"I thought you were on vacation."

"Well, not exactly. I'll explain later, but I need to speak to Massimo."

"He's not here."

"Where is he?"

"He said he's coming in late. He's having breakfast."

"With his mistress?"

"No, with his wife, for a change. He came this close to blowing up his marriage. If I hadn't called to warn him his wife was on her way home last Friday, he would be thrown out on the streets and we'd be thrown out of a job."

"Gerda, this is an emergency. I need him to get to Venice as fast as he can, to this address." Hadley made Gerda repeat the address.

"What's this about?"

"There's no time to explain, but I need him to get here right away."

"I'll track him down and make the arrangements," Gerda said.

"Gerda, are you okay?"

"Of course. Why do you ask?"

"Well you were just at the doctor last week and the temp said you went back today. Is there something you're not telling me?"

"Everything's fine. Nothing to worry about."

"But I do worry. If you're sick—"

"We'll talk about it when you get back to Florence. And, I almost forgot, there's someone named Charles King looking for you."

"King Charles?"

"Maybe I got the name mixed up, but he was here this morning. He just flew in, and I didn't want to give him your address without checking with you first."

"Damn."

"He says he's your boyfriend."

"You didn't tell him about Luca, did you?"

"Of course not. I didn't give him any personal information, just that you are on vacation."

Hadley breathed a sigh of relief. *But what unfortunate timing.* Charles hadn't visited her the entire six months she'd attended classes in Florence or during the time she'd been working at her new job. And now, of all times, when she was in the middle of a crisis, he shows up?

"And your mother has been calling," Gerda added. "She says you aren't answering your phone."

The gears in Hadley's head were spinning out of control, and her radar was on high alert. Somehow, her mother had something to do with this new development.

Hadley dialed her mother's cell phone.

"Mom. I heard you wanted to talk to me."

"I was just thinking it's been a while since we've

heard from you."

Something was definitely up. Her mother was being too casual.

"I've been busy at work, and I, um, went to Venice this week. I'm actually still here."

"Venice, but—you need to get back to Florence. You're not with that Italian boy, are you?"

"His name is Luca, Mother. And we're here on business."

"Monkey business?"

"No, he's helping me on a case." Hadley fought to get her breathing under control. "Mom, have you heard from Charles lately?"

"Charles?"

"Yes, Charles King. Mother, what aren't you telling me?"

Her mother hesitated. "I was sworn to secrecy."

"You know you can't keep a secret. What's going on?"

"Charles is on his way to Florence. In fact, his plane has probably just landed."

"Why is he coming here now, when he refused to visit me for a whole year?"

"It's a surprise."

"Well, the cat's out of the bag. What is he doing in Florence?"

"He's going to propose."

Hadley drew in a deep breath.

"I hoped he would propose before I left for Florence, but he didn't. He didn't want me to go, but he wouldn't make a commitment. And he hasn't bothered to visit me all this time because he's mad that I left. So what's the sudden rush?"

"I might have told him about Luca."

"You *might* have told him?"

"I said it was just a fling, nothing serious. But I think he just wants to stake his claim."

"Mother, this isn't a gold rush."

This is bad, Hadley thought. *Very bad.*

"He bought a ring. He asked your father and me for our blessing, and he showed us the stone. It's beautiful."

Hadley started to hyperventilate.

"Mother, I can't think about this now. I wish you wouldn't have interfered, or at least you could have warned me."

"I'm not interfering. Are you planning to stay in Italy the rest of your life and live with that Italian? You need to come home and settle down. Charles dropped out of law school."

"I heard about that."

"He's miserable without you."

"Are you blaming me because he dropped out of law school?"

"Nobody's blaming anyone. It's just that he's been wandering around the campus bookstore looking for a Master's degree major. He started with the A's and he's rejected Accounting, Biology, Chemistry and Dental Sciences. He's landed on the E's. I think he's planning to major in Economics."

"Well I wish him luck, but I'm exactly where I want to be. If he was so in love with me, he'd have made the effort to be with me."

"Well, he's making the effort now."

"I've moved on," Hadley announced.

"With your Italian lover?"

Well, yes, maybe.

"With my life. I love living in Italy. But Mother, I have to go now. I'll call you when I get back to Florence."

Hadley felt the mother of all headaches coming on. What was Rule Number Six of Massimo's Pocket Guide? Don't Panic In A Crisis. This predicament certainly qualified as a crisis. And she was definitely panicking. What if something was wrong with Gerda? She'd been like a second mother to Hadley. If anything should happen to her, well, she couldn't go there right now. The curator was on her way to the villa, and Hadley wasn't prepared. She was doubting herself and her decision to take on this case alone. Luca was missing in action, and she had to face Matteo, masquerading as mini-Göring, by herself. And King Charles was in Florence. She was a circus juggler trying to keep all the balls in the air and failing spectacularly. All her secrets and lies were beginning to catch up with her.

Chapter Thirteen

Hadley walked along the Grand Canal, breathing in the familiar sights and sounds. Venice life was beginning to come alive—the noises of vaporetto traffic, the insistent sound of church bells, the lapping of water against the docks, the appearance of residents and tourists about to start their day in this fabulous city, one of her favorites in the country.

She was well on her way to violating Massimo's Rule Number Five. She had arrived at the villa without a plan. She couldn't just knock on the door. Matteo might be home. Where was Luca? Where was Massimo? And where was the elusive Uffizi curator whose name she didn't even know?

Luca materialized behind her, and she jumped.

"I didn't mean to scare you."

"Where did you go this morning?"

"Out for a walk, to do some thinking."

Hadley frowned. "And did that walk include visiting Isabella?"

"I walked by the villa to see if I could determine whether her brother was home."

"And?"

"He hasn't left the house."

"How long have you been here?"

"A few hours."

"Are you crazy?"

"I just thought…in case Isabella needed me."

Hadley shook her head. "What if I needed you?"

"You kicked me out of your bed, remember?"

Hadley tried to look remorseful. "I let you sleep on the couch, but obviously, you haven't slept. Have you eaten?"

"No," Luca said.

Hadley reached into her handbag and removed what was left of the croissant. She handed him the napkin.

He unwrapped the pastry and raised his brows.

"Looks like an animal got into this."

"No, it was me. I bit off the top."

Luca laughed. "I'm starving, so I'm going to eat this anyway."

"It was yours, but you weren't there, so…"

"Cara," he whispered. "I'm sorry."

"For what?"

"For whatever it is you think I've done. Are we good now?"

"I haven't decided."

"Well, let me know when you make up your mind."

"Meanwhile—" Luca leaned over and kissed her full on the mouth, branding her. "You taste like honey, amore mio."

"I dipped the croissant into some honey before I ate it."

"Very generous of you to share," he said, piercing her with his eyes as he brought her body toward his.

A booming voice erupted out of the mist from behind them.

"Hadley. I'm here. What's the emergency? What are you doing in Venice?"

Hadley broke away from Luca to face her boss.

"Massimo, thank you for coming."

"Luca, it's nice to see you again."

"You too, Signore Domingo."

Hadley twisted her hands and shifted her weight from her left foot to her right.

"You know Rule Number Seven in your *Pocket Guide*?"

"Of course. Don't Be Afraid To Ask for Help."

"Well, I'm afraid I'm in way over my head. I thought I could handle this situation, but—"

"Handle what situation?"

Hadley exhaled. "Last Friday, when you were, um, indisposed, I mean at lunch with, well, unavailable, I got a phone call, and I didn't want to bother you. I thought I could handle things by myself. That I would bring in a new client for the agency."

"What new client?"

"A woman. A woman who claimed she was the new curator for the Uffizi Gallery."

"There is no new curator at the Uffizi. The current curator is a man."

"Yes, I have since discovered that, but this woman—"

"Does this woman have a name?"

"Well, that's the thing. I met with her last Friday night at Piazzale Michelangelo. She gave me her card, but there was no name on the card, just a phone number."

"And what did she want?"

"She said that a Botticelli study sent to an exhibit at the High Museum in Atlanta indicated that either the study was a fake, or that possibly *Birth of Venus* in the Uffizi is a fake."

"That's impossible," Massimo barked. "That

Botticelli is not a fake."

"That's what I thought. But the study, the face of Venus, looked nothing like the artist model in *Birth of Venus*. And now I know why. It is a study of a completely different Botticelli painting called *Amore*. It's the third in his trilogy."

"Hadley, there is no third Botticelli painting. There's only *Birth of Venus* and *Primavera*."

"But, Massimo—Signore Domingo, I saw it with my own eyes. It's called *Amore*, it's brilliant, executed in the same style as his other two masterpieces."

"But that's impossible. If there was a third piece, we would know about it."

Hadley rushed the words, tripping over the sentences to get out the story of the frightened girl locked in the villa, and the secret museum where the paintings were hidden away, and the diary documenting the provenance of *Amore*.

"Slow down, Hadley." Are you saying you saw a third Botticelli in this villa, right here in Venice?"

"Certo," she answered. "And there were more besides, smaller Botticellis and other masters, paintings I've never heard of or seen before. And crates of others locked away in storage in the same villa."

Massimo became animated. "This could be a find of a lifetime. A lost masterpiece. But what led you to this villa?"

"The woman."

"Ah, the mystery woman with no name."

"She's going to meet us here this morning. In fact, I'm expecting her at any minute."

"How did this woman know where to find these particular paintings?"

"She gave me this address, so Luca and I came here and met the owner of the villa, who let us into a locked museum."

"How do you know this woman is not an art thief?"

"That's it. I don't know anything. I've begun to suspect something isn't right, which is why I called you. The woman was acting suspiciously. She's on her way with a team to collect the art."

"Collect the art? She must not do that. I'm right, she's an art thief. What does this woman look like?"

Luca stepped up. "Signore, I took a picture of her at the Piazza that evening. Here, I'll show you." Luca took out his camera and located the photo he'd shot of the woman.

Massimo studied the photo intently. "It's rather dark. But this young woman looks familiar." Massimo rubbed his chin. "If I'm not mistaken, this is Ingrid Adelman. She's the last surviving relative of a family that was wiped out in the Holocaust. Over the past eighty years, her family has been trying to get restitution or the return of their property, including priceless works of art. They haven't had much success to date.

"Some of their paintings were restored from public museums and private individuals around the world who weren't aware they were stolen, but governments were rarely cooperative, and the family lost their cases more often than they won. But I wasn't involved in finding a Botticelli painting. Apparently, the biggest prize of them all managed to elude them.

"None of the museums in Germany or Austria are cooperating. She's had some luck with the U.S. Attorney and the FBI in New York when they were able to retrieve a looted painting from a museum or a private citizen. But the bulk of the family's fortune has figuratively gone up in smoke. Lost forever. She may be trying an end run, having us track down some of the paintings on her behalf. I worked with her father but was unable to find more than one or two of the looted paintings. She probably got my name from him and hoped I could circumvent the courts."

"Isn't that illegal?"

"Not if she can prove the paintings belonged to her family."

"I have a diary, and I know where the Botticelli studies are that may be able to verify the provenance of the lost masterpiece."

"But I wonder, was she just going to steal the paintings? You say she's bringing a team?"

"I told her to bring crates, lots of crates. But Signore, there may be a problem."

"What kind of problem?"

"One of the owners of the villa is the grandson of Hermann Göring. His sister says he's violent. These paintings have been hidden away for a long time. He has secretly been selling them off, but even if we get in, he will not allow us to take them."

"Luca, have you contacted the Carabinieri Art Squad?"

"No, Hadley asked me not to."

"Well, I'll need to get into the villa to see the paintings myself. We'll have to formulate a plan before we decide how to proceed."

"Rule Number Five," Hadley offered.

"Esattamente." Massimo beamed.

"No wonder she was so secretive. She wasn't being honest with me."

"The art detective world is shady," Massimo admitted.

"What rule is that?"

"Perhaps that will be the first rule in Book Two of my *Pocket Guide*."

"Are you working on Book Two?"

"I had every intention, but life has gotten in the way."

A girl in a blonde ponytail got off a vaporetto and strode toward them.

"That's the girl, the curator imposter," Hadley noted.

"Ah, yes, that's Miss Adelman. She's trying to regain possession of her stolen property with or without the courts. Can't say as I blame her."

Hadley stepped closer to Massimo. "She thinks you've been working the case with me the whole time."

"Understood." Massimo stepped forward and took Ingrid's hand.

"Miss Adelman, it's a pleasure to meet you. I enjoyed working with your grandmother and your father."

"Yes, he was very impressed with you and how you helped him with the return of some of our paintings. But that was just the tip of the iceberg."

"So you decided to take matters into your own hands, bypass the courts."

Ingrid bristled. "You know our history. The court is of little use in these matters. They tend to protect the ill-gotten gains of the looters."

"True in many cases," Massimo admitted. "Some subsequent owners aren't even aware of where their paintings came from. But there's a right way and a wrong way to win the day."

"Rule Number Eight in *Massimo Domingo's Guide to Stolen Art Recovery*," Hadley pointed out, removing the olive-oil stained *Pocket Guide* from her handbag and opening it to the eighth chapter.

"What I mean by that is that you stoop to the level of the art thieves if you simply try to steal back your paintings," Massimo pointed out.

"*My* paintings," Ingrid insisted. "Both my father and my grandmother died before our property was restored. I don't intend to do the same."

"My dear, you need more than good intentions in the art detective business," Massimo pontificated.

"Rule Number Nine," offered Hadley.

"Frankly, Signore, I'm tired of playing by the rules. I know my property is here. This villa was sold under duress by my grandfather, and I'll wager the paintings 'acquired' with it are here as well. I've done my research, and I won't be swayed. I'm tired of waiting for what's mine."

"If I took the Germans to court, they would win," Ingrid pointed out, "even if the lawsuit originated in the United States."

She was no doubt correct. Massimo explained to Luca and Hadley that in August 2020 a U.S. federal appeals court in Los Angeles ruled that a painting estimated at $30 million, traded to the Nazis by a Jewish woman wanting to escape the Holocaust in 1939, could remain the property of the Spanish museum that acquired it in 1992. So the Thyssen-Bornemisza Museum in Madrid was allowed to keep the Impressionist painting, *Rue St.-Honoré, Apres-Midi, Effet de Pluie,* painted in 1897 by Camille Pissarro.

"This case cycled through the courts of Spain and the United States for twenty years," explained Ingrid. "That woman inherited the painting from her father-in-law. We have proof of that because she had a photo of her family with the painting. In 1939 she traded it to the Nazis in exchange for exit visas for herself, her husband, and her grandson. The heirs spent years trying to recover the painting, finally concluding it was lost and accepting $13,000 in reparations from the German government. The painting was hanging in the family's German home. I have such a picture of my great-grandparents with one of the paintings here, standing in front of *Amore*."

Massimo added, "This is just one more example of a Jewish family denied its legacy by a museum that won't return the looted art. Of course, she can appeal, but that's not always successful."

Hadley mentioned another famous case that did have a happy ending. She cited the eventual return of "The Lady in Gold," the 1907 Gustav Klimt painting *Portrait of Adele Bloch-Bauer I*, worth $135 million and displayed at the Galerie Belvedere in Vienna.

The painting, commissioned and owned by Bauer's husband, a Jewish banker and sugar producer, was stolen by the Nazis in 1941 and confiscated with his property and assets when he fled to Switzerland. Upon his death in 1946, he designated his nieces and nephew to inherit his estate. It was finally returned to Adele Block-Bauer's niece and bought by Ronald Lauder for his Neue Galerie, New York. Hadley had seen the painting—oil, silver, and gold on canvas, representative of Klimt's golden phase—on display in person in New York. She had stood mesmerized by the painting, just as she had done when she first set eyes on *Amore*. There were other Klimts at the Belvedere, but none so exquisite.

"But that was a long and tedious seven-year process. I have already spent most of my adult life trying to seek justice."

"Well, let's knock on the door and see what's on the other side," Massimo asserted, in an effort to maintain decorum.

"Luca, why don't you do the honors. Let's make this an official visit."

Luca nodded, pulled out his badge and knocked on the door. His gun was visible to all.

For a minute no one answered, but there was definite movement inside the villa. The locks unclicked, and the door opened.

"Luca," Isabella stepped forward until she saw the other people. "Who are all these people?"

"These are people who are here to help. Isabella, you remember Hadley Evans, and this is her boss, Signore Massimo Domingo from Firenze. And this is Signorina Ingrid Adelman."

"I appreciate you all coming, but my brother, Matteo, will be back soon, and he can't find you all here."

"I've been guarding the door. He didn't come out."

"There's a secret entrance in the back. He slips in and out anytime he pleases."

Luca reached out and skimmed the back of his hand lightly across Isabella's neck. She recoiled.

"Did Matteo hurt you?"

Isabella quickly covered the front of her lowcut dress with a sweater.

"And here?" Luca swore and raised his voice, while he pulled back the sweater. Dark purple bruises bloomed across her breasts and the front of her neck.

The key was no longer around Isabella's neck.

Tears welled in Isabella's eyes. "When he found out you were here yesterday, he lost his temper, again." She covered her face in shame.

Luca tipped Isabella's chin up with his finger so they were face to face. "Isabella, this isn't normal behavior. I cannot tolerate it. I'm taking you away from here. No arguments."

Hadley's thoughts whirled. Where was he planning to take Isabella? Back to Florence? To his house? Why did he have to be her savior? He looked like he wanted to kiss her bruises away. And where did Hadley fit into this cozy scenario?

"We're here to see the paintings," Hadley began, trying to take control of a deteriorating situation.

"Matteo took the key to the museum. He said I could no longer be trusted."

Luca swept past Isabella. The others followed. "I don't need a key," he bellowed.

"What are you going to do?" Hadley asked.

"Shoot off the lock if I have to, or break down the door."

"Luca, no! Matteo will know you've been here. It's too dangerous. He plans to remove the paintings today. To sell them. You all need to leave right away."

Luca frowned. "I'm not afraid of a bully."

Ingrid wrung her hands in bewilderment. Massimo looked proudly at Luca. "Lead the way, my boy."

Luca led them up the stairs to the museum entrance. He tried the door handle. It wouldn't budge. "Stand back," Luca yelled. He pulled out his pistol and shot off the lock. He strode in, and the group followed, assembling in the center of the circular room.

Hadley switched on the light. Massimo was the first to react. "Oh, mio Dio." He couldn't tear his eyes away from *Amore*.

Ingrid sobbed, belying her cool exterior demeanor. "It's *Amore*." With trembling fingers, she opened her purse and pulled out a crinkled, faded, black-and-white photograph. "Here are my grandparents standing in front of this painting in their home in Berlin. Proof that *Amore* belongs to our family. No one believed me when I told them about the third Botticelli, but here, you see. It's true."

"If I didn't see this with my own eyes, I wouldn't believe it," Massimo agreed, speaking reverently upon closer examination. "It's a lost masterpiece."

"Is it genuine?" Hadley asked.

"There's no doubt," answered the signore. "Unsigned. Even further proof. And if we can authenticate the diary, we have our documentation."

"Where has this painting been hiding all these centuries?" Hadley wondered.

"The possibilities are endless," Massimo said. "Tracing the provenance will be difficult. But as to how it came to be here, I would guess it changed hands during the war. Ingrid, do you have any idea about the provenance of the painting?"

"No," she said, "except that the last *legitimate* owner was my grandfather."

"Herr Adelman."

"Yes."

"There's one possible theory," Massimo speculated. "World War Two unleashed a tsunami of devastation across the continent. When the Allies began bombing

Berlin, Hitler ordered the construction of three 'impenetrable' flak towers to safeguard the city's art treasures and those he had 'acquired' by illegal means. These included seven hundred works of art by some of the world's great masters—Caravaggio, Donatello, Rubens, and three of Botticelli's early religious works— four hundred paintings and three hundred sculptures in all. One of these towers—Flakturm Friedrichshain—was the evacuation site for what is today known as the Bode-Museum.

"In May 1945, the Soviets attacked the city and snatched up any works of art they could find, taking approximately two million objects worth billions of dollars," Massimo continued. "Two suspicious fires broke out, and three floors of the tower being used by the museum were burned, and all the contents were believed destroyed.

"Many believe the Soviets were responsible for starting the fires to cover up their theft of the treasures they had taken or that they may have pilfered some of the masterpieces before the second fire struck. Many people think these precious works of art may not really have been destroyed.

"Many years later, a Botticelli painting thought to be part of the burned collection surfaced at auction, proving it had survived the blaze. There was hope that others did too. As you know, Botticelli is best known for two of his mythological works—*The Birth of Venus* and *Primavera*—but this is the third, only rumored, until now. What a groundbreaking discovery! A great mystery.

"What if Göring managed to wrest it from the Russians? That would explain why it wasn't at Carinhall, but why didn't it end up with the rest of the recovered paintings after his arrest?"

"In her diary, Göring's mistress, Isabella's grandmother, said he was hiding it from Hitler," Hadley explained. "It was that valuable. He never displayed it at Carinhall. And, according to the diary, he 'acquired' it indirectly from Ingrid's grandfather, so it probably never made it to the museum and then to the flak tower. It would make sense that he stored it away from the other paintings. He had this special museum built in the villa to hide it."

"And look around, Signore, at the other paintings in the room," Hadley said.

Massimo literally had to force himself to tear his eyes away from *Amore*. He studied the paintings, some Botticellis, others by similar Italian masters.

"It's a treasure trove." He turned to Isabella. "And you say there's more in crates hidden in this villa?"

Isabella nodded.

"And Signore, remember your Rule Number Three, Always Look Beneath the Surface," Hadley said, pointing to the large framed piece of art hanging across from *Amore.* "I think upon closer inspection you may uncover another masterpiece beneath this canvas."

Massimo moved toward the painting, examined it, and concluded, "You may be right."

"It might take years to catalog these, trace the provenance, and find their rightful owners, if that's even possible," observed Massimo. "Many European countries will be vying for these, trying to claim them. We could be tied up in court for decades."

Ingrid sighed. "Now you see what I've been going through."

"Miss Adelman, I will make every effort to restore your property to you, no matter how long it takes."

Ingrid looked relieved.

"What about this villa? Does it belong to your family?"

"It does," Ingrid said.

Isabella twisted her hands. "This is my home."

The tension in the room was as thick as a blanket of fog.

No one noticed the presence of another man in the room.

"This is my house, and you are trespassing."

Isabella gasped and stepped back in alarm. "Matteo!"

He shot his sister a menacing scowl.

"You let these people in again, after I told you not to? Did you not learn your lesson? I'll deal with you later." He dismissed her as if she were a pesky gnat. Then he addressed the rest of the people in the room. "Now, if you don't leave my property, I will call the *polizia*."

"I *am* the police," said Luca, stepping up and flashing his badge. "I don't have much use for men who use women as their personal punching bags. You belong in jail for what you've done to your sister."

Isabella looked down at the marble floor.

"What goes on in the privacy of my home is no business of yours. You need to leave immediately. I have some important guests arriving shortly."

"Matteo, you know we are forbidden from selling those paintings. Grandmother always told us—"

"And what did our grandmother expect us to live on? What funds did she leave us to maintain this villa? Our grandmother was a whore. She was bought and paid for, and everything in this villa belongs to me. What do you think has been supporting us all these years? I give you people fair warning. Your plans to divvy up my family's legacy are premature—everybody out!" Matteo ordered.

Luca reholstered his gun, grabbed Matteo by his shirt, and lifted him off the ground.

"I represent the Carabinieri. These paintings do not belong to you. They are stolen property. Distribution of these assets will be left to the authorities. I am officially notifying you that we will be taking possession of the looted contents in this villa. You may stay and cooperate or you may vacate the villa. Your choice." He dropped Matteo unceremoniously, and he stumbled but managed to remain upright.

"I will call my lawyers," said Matteo.

"Call them," Luca challenged. "And your sister will bring assault charges against you."

Isabella became agitated. Matteo moved toward his sister, grabbed a hank of her long blonde hair and pulled her up tightly against him.

"This is all your fault. You let these strangers into my house and ruined all my plans. You just can't follow orders."

Matteo took out a knife and held it against his sister's throat, teasing out a spot of blood.

"I swear I will kill her if you don't all leave," Matteo threatened.

Isabella froze.

Luca went for his weapon, itching to use it. "Just give me a reason."

"Luca, don't," Isabella cried. "He won't hurt me. I'm his sister. He loves me."

"He's already hurt you," Luca reasoned softly, his eyes never leaving hers. Focusing like a laser on Matteo, he raised his voice to her captor. "Let her go, or I will have no choice but to use this weapon."

"I hold all the cards," Matteo cackled. "This villa and all its contents belong to me. It was gifted to my grandmother and passed down to my mother and then me."

"And your sister," Luca mentioned.

"She will do as I say. Her opinion is of no value."

"Sir," Massimo said, stepping forward. "We can resolve this peacefully. No one needs to get hurt. We have a woman here who claims she's the proper owner of this painting and perhaps others in the house. The courts will have to weigh in."

"I've already made arrangements for *Amore* and the rest of the paintings to be picked up today by buyers, so I'm afraid the matter is out of your hands."

Hadley felt a headache coming on. She feared for Isabella and for Luca. If Luca shot Matteo, he would be committing a crime. If not, and Matteo carried out his threat, his sister would be the victim. Isabella didn't deserve to die. Something had to be done to break the stalemate. She reached into her purse and pulled out a metal nail file.

"If you harm your sister, I will slash this painting and it won't be worth anything to anyone."

Matteo frowned, slightly loosening his hold on Isabella. His eyes flew to the painting. "You wouldn't dare."

"I would," Hadley swore.

"Hadley," Massimo said, calmly. "You don't want to ruin that masterpiece. It's invaluable."

"So is Isabella's life," she stated.

"Matteo, we can talk this over, come to an agreement," Luca said, straining to control his anger.

Hadley held up the nail file and approached the masterpiece.

"Hadley, don't!" Massimo shouted.

Hadley's hands shook. Would she do it? Could she destroy the most beautiful work of art she'd ever seen? And if she did attempt to damage the masterpiece, would Luca shoot her, or Matteo throw the knife at her first? If it meant saving a life, maybe two, she would have no choice.

"Let her go," Luca urged, raising his gun. "Hadley, step away from the painting."

"Hadley," Isabella pleaded. "Don't ruin the painting. That was our grandmother's legacy."

Matteo's glazed eyes were fixed on Hadley and the painting. He seemed to have momentarily forgotten about his sister.

Suddenly, Isabella swirled around and turned the knife in her brother's hand down and across, plunging it deep into Matteo's ribs.

"Enough. I've had enough," she shouted. When she saw the blood staining Matteo's shirt, she dropped the knife and ran to Luca. In shock, she went pale, and her eyes rolled back in her head.

Luca caught her in his arms.

Hadley exhaled and placed the nail file carefully back in her purse, sharp end down. Her heartbeat slowed.

"Hadley, were you really going to destroy that precious work of art?" Massimo asked.

"N-no," she stammered uncertainly. "I don't think so, but I had to do something."

Matteo clutched his stomach. Massimo pulled out his phone and made an emergency call.

"The ambulance will be here in a few minutes," he announced.

Hadley looked at Luca, who had carried Isabella over to the viewing bench in the center of the room and was cradling her in his arms. Luca seemed lost in Isabella. Was he lost to her? He had risked his life to save the girl. He was in full hero mode. Would he have risked his life for anyone, or was Isabella the woman he truly cared for? When Hadley saw Luca with the gun pointed at Matteo, she had been so frightened for him, frantic about how the scene would play out.

She realized, at that moment, she was in love with him. But was it too late? And what about King Charles? He was waiting for her back in Florence. She had to face him. Maybe it would all work out for the best. Luca with Isabella—both comfortably Italian and culturally compatible, and King Charles with her. Two fish out of European waters.

The ambulance arrived, and the emergency medical technicians picked up Matteo and began working on him. Another medic examined Isabella, who had begun to come to.

"She's had quite a shock," Luca said. "It's a classic case of abuse. Check out her bruises as well."

"Will you be accompanying the patients to hospital?" one of the medics asked Luca.

Luca looked at Hadley.

"It's okay," she said, defeated. "Go with her. Make sure she's okay."

While the medics put Matteo's stretcher in the back of the ambulance, Luca helped Isabella into the front seat.

Massimo turned to Hadley. "I'll call the Art Squad. I have my contact numbers back at the office. I'll get them from Gerda."

Hadley blushed and handed over the little black notebook to her boss. "I have your contact book, Signore. I'm sorry. I took it from your desk. I thought I might need it."

Massimo didn't hesitate. "You did the right thing."

"You're not mad at me?"

"Why would I be mad? Your actions will right many wrongs."

Ingrid walked over and stood in front of the painting. She held out her cell phone. "Here, Hadley, take a picture of me in front of *Amore*. I want to send this to my attorney."

Hadley took the shot.

"I only wish my father and my grandmother were alive to see this. After so long, we may finally have it back."

"You look exhausted, Hadley," Massimo said. "I am on the job now. I understand you have out-of-town company. Why don't we wait for the Art Squad, make sure the paintings are photographed and protected and shipped to a warehouse in Florence where we can access and inspect them. Then we'll do our best to get them into the right hands. You can help me do a preliminary catalog of the works. I'll take over your hotel room. You can make the afternoon train back to Florence tonight, so you won't keep your young man waiting." By "young man," Hadley knew Massimo was talking about King Charles and not Luca. Even he could see that Luca was no longer hers.

She hated to leave at such a critical juncture, but she knew she had to resolve the state of affairs with King Charles. And she didn't want to stick around to witness the blossoming romance between Luca and Isabella.

"Did I ever tell you about the time when—" Massimo began.

"Actually," Hadley interrupted, sure she'd heard his story a dozen times before, "Ingrid looks as if she could use some nourishment. Why don't I take her down to Piazza San Marco to get something to eat and clear her head?"

"That would be wonderful," Ingrid said, relief in her eyes.

Ingrid looked like she could use some fritto misto and a friend.

"Miss Adelman, rest assured I will do right by you," Massimo assured. "When you and Hadley return, you are welcome to wait here with us, or you can return to wherever it is you came from. We will make sure the proper paperwork is filed."

"I'd prefer to wait here with *Amore*, if I might. But I would love a break."

"You're welcome to wait, but you understand it could take months to sort this all out."

"My family has already waited more than eighty years. Another few months won't make a difference."

Hadley stretched her arms and followed Massimo around while he did his job. He really was good at this. It had probably been so long since he'd had such a high-profile case, he'd lost his way. But he was gaining his footing, in his element, and she was happy to be at his side.

She longed for the familiar, for stability. She even

missed her mother. Maybe it was time to give up her dreams and go home.

Chapter Fourteen

Hadley and Ingrid snagged a prime outdoor table at St. Mark's Square. It was a touristy establishment and the pigeons were out in force, but it was a beautiful day, and they were enjoying the ambience only Venice can offer. And you could hardly get a bad meal in Italy. Hadley ordered an amaretto sour, and Ingrid was sipping a Bellini. It was a little early in the afternoon to be drinking, but Hadley felt she'd already lived a lifetime in a day, and she was still steaming over Luca's behavior.

"I'm sorry I lied to you and pretended I was a museum curator," Ingrid said. "But it was the only way I could get the help I needed. I had exhausted the court system. I didn't have enough evidence."

Hadley knew a thing or two about lying, so how could she not accept Ingrid's apology?

"I was certain you were going to be my pathway to a job at the Uffizi."

"Is that what you want out of life?" Ingrid asked. She seemed really interested.

"Sure, why not?" What she really wanted was Luca, but that vaporetto had already left the lagoon. "If you're not a museum curator, then what are you?"

"A math teacher."

Hadley laughed. "About as far away from art history as possible."

"But I love art. Paintings were prized in my family."

"Can you tell me the story?" Hadley prompted, "If you're ready?"

The server placed a large order of fritto misto and two Caprese salads at the table and then refilled their water glasses. Apparently, the two women had more in common than art. They had the same taste in food. If they had met under different circumstances, quite by chance, Hadley thought they could be good friends.

"If you tell me what's going on between you and that hot cop of yours." The tension in the air was as thick as molasses.

"He's not mine, not anymore. We were dating, and then along came Isabella, and it was love at first sight."

"He wasn't looking at her the way he was looking at you," Ingrid observed.

"Well, then I think you need to have your eyes checked."

"I can see what's right in front of me. I'm quite sure he's yours, if you want him."

Hadley was eager to change the subject. "I'd rather not talk about it."

As they ate their lunch, which was delicious, Ingrid told her story despite the fact that thousands of tourists swarmed the square around them.

"My grandfather came from a long line of wealthy bankers. They lived in a big house in Berlin, and he was an avid art collector. Unfortunately, he used the same Swiss art dealer as Hermann Göring, and that's where the trouble started.

"It was way before they enacted the racist and antisemitic Nuremberg laws, and before Kristallnacht. They had just opened Dachau, the first Nazi concentration camp, in 1933 in southern Germany. At the beginning, it was a camp for political prisoners, Communists and Marxists, before it became a death camp. Ostensibly, the inmates would be implementing land cultivation projects. But it was really a forced labor camp and a place where Jews as well as German and Austrian criminals were imprisoned, and eventually foreign nationals from occupied countries were added. No visitors were allowed.

"When Göring learned that my grandfather had acquired *Amore*, he had the gallery owner intercede, but my grandfather would not give up his treasure for anything, so they sent him to Dachau for several months to persuade him to see things their way.

"My grandmother, who by then had a young son, my father, was frantic. Her husband was taken away in the middle of the night, and she didn't know if she'd ever see him again. Prisoners at Dachau were terrorized and brutalized. My grandfather was a gentle man, with no political leanings, certainly not a Communist or a Marxist. He didn't fit any of the categories. But then, the Nazis didn't play by the rules. He had something they wanted, so they made an example of him.

"My grandmother was terrified. She wanted to leave Germany right away, leave everything behind, but she wouldn't leave without my grandfather. And his whole family was there—parents, brothers, aunts, uncles, cousins. One night, without advance notice, my grandfather walked in the door, and he and my grandmother embraced. My father remembers that my grandmother was in tears, so happy to have him back, and that she nearly didn't let him go. He was emaciated. He'd been worked to near death and starvation.

" 'We must leave,' said my grandmother. 'I'm

already packed.' But my grandfather, despite what he'd just been through, refused. He didn't want to part with *Amore*, but he was warned if he didn't give up the painting, his life and the lives of his family couldn't be guaranteed.

" 'I'll give them what they want and they'll leave us alone. We are first and foremost Germans. We belong here. This is our home.' Despite what they'd put him through, he was still proud to be a German citizen.

"My grandfather sold *Amore* back to the gallery owner at a fraction of its value, and they continued to live in Berlin until 1940. Each year, restrictions on Jews got tighter and tighter, until the stranglehold and isolation was complete. My grandfather had to trade more paintings for his family's safety.

"My grandmother begged him to reconsider and leave Germany, but by the time my grandfather saw the handwriting on the wall, it was too late. My grandfather contacted the gallery owner to negotiate. His goal was to attain safe passage out of Berlin for himself and his family. But he paid a heavy price. He arranged to sell his property, his fine home in Berlin, his business holdings, for a fraction of their worth. At the time, property rights of Jews were rarely respected. He unloaded the remainder of his paintings, even his vacation villa in Venice. He still thought of himself as a German, even though the Germans didn't want him.

"Finally, he received the proper documentation to leave Germany. He insisted my grandmother and my father go to the ship, and he would be close behind with the last of their luggage. My grandmother took dozens of family pictures from their home, of my grandfather dressed in his suit and a tallit, his prayer shawl, their wedding photograph, pictures of my father growing up, and her silver candlesticks. I still have them.

"So the family emigrated to America?" Hadley asked, as she munched on her fried calamari.

"My grandfather was able to get only two travel visas. He didn't have the heart to tell my grandmother. My grandmother and father waited and waited on the top deck of the ship they were to sail on, and when the ship pulled away, she thought he had somehow boarded without her notice. When she reviewed the documents on the ship, she realized there were only two names on the paperwork. Hers and my father's. My grandfather was never coming. The extra luggage did make it onto the ship. But my grandfather didn't. I imagine he brought the rest of the luggage and saw them searching frantically for him and kept them in sight until the vessel pulled away. She never saw her husband again.

"When they arrived safely in America, they contacted dozens of government agencies, the Red Cross, and Jewish immigration organizations but didn't find out until the end of the war that my grandfather had been rounded up just days after the ship departed and that he had perished in Auschwitz along with his entire family."

"How horrible," Hadley whispered. "The Germans broke their promise."

"It's what they do."

"Why didn't all the Jews just leave?"

"Ah. That is the first question many people ask. But you must understand, they didn't know what was coming. It didn't happen all at once. It was gradual. The rules, the restrictions, the ridicule, the roundups, the beatings, the burning of books and shops and synagogues and eventually the mass murder. Like my grandfather, the Jews all thought they were German first. That something like this could never happen in their country."

"Well, couldn't you go back to Berlin now and reclaim your house, your grandfather's business?"

Ingrid shook her head. "It sounds so easy, but we would be tied up in courts for years, and there are no guarantees. There was nothing to go home to. All our family's assets, including the paintings, had been appropriated along with the property and given to others by the state, so we were no longer the legal owners. Someone else is living in that house now, and they won't readily give it up. Most of the families like mine never survived to make a claim.

"Our paintings have been auctioned and bought and sold privately, changing hands for the past eight decades, assets that rightly belonged to our branch of the family that managed to make it to the United States. The provenance of the artwork has become murky, and we have been unsuccessfully seeking justice, restitution, and the recovery of our property and priceless paintings since the end of the war.

"Now I am the only one left. Second generation. The Claims Conference dispenses minimal funds for all those who went underground, were on the run or in hiding, or who lost their lives in a ghetto, a labor camp, or a death camp, or had their lives disrupted from 1933-1945. Those who escaped are considered survivors, and we have to bear witness. I have dedicated my whole life to getting restitution for my grandfather. My grandmother and my father are no longer alive to see this day, but I will fight till my dying breath for them.

"I don't do it for the money," Ingrid explained. "I do

it because they were living, breathing people with real hopes and dreams. They didn't deserve the treatment they got. My grandmother never remarried. She and my father felt guilty that they were spared and my grandfather wasn't, that he gave up everything so they could live. I've spent my life trying to make sense of it. I'm a mathematician, and still, it doesn't add up."

By this time Ingrid was crying openly, so Hadley reached across the table and held Ingrid's hand in hers. "Eat your calamari before it gets cold," was all she could manage, but she vowed she would help Ingrid in her crusade to right the wrongs of the past, to do her small part in restoring balance to the world.

Chapter Fifteen

Hadley reached her apartment at twilight. She hadn't been able to sleep on the train. The stars in the evening sky were beginning to brighten in the inky darkness. Florence was magical at any time of day. Her stomach growled. She hadn't eaten since she and Ingrid had shared a light snack in the café.

There hadn't been time for a proper meal with all the recovery work to be done at the villa. They'd gotten word that Matteo would need surgery but that his outlook was positive. She hadn't heard from Luca, so she supposed he was still with Isabella. No news about whether she would file charges against her brother, or whether she'd be charged for attempted murder, or what would become of the siblings now that Ingrid had made clear her intention to seek restitution for the property in Venice. Isabella was only defending herself. She was sure Luca would make it right.

When she arrived, she found a sleeping figure slouched against the door. King Charles was snoring deeply. She studied him in repose. He was as good-looking as she remembered him, not as handsome or as tall as Luca but still well-built. It had been a year since they'd seen each other. She felt… She didn't know how she felt, not ambivalent, but her heart was not racing.

Hadley shook him gently awake.

"Charles, I'm home," she said softly.

Still in a daze, Charles smiled at her through hooded eyes. When he tried to get up, he was stiff and wobbly, but once he got his bearings he jumped up.

"Hadley," he exclaimed. "Boy, I've missed you. I should have come sooner."

Then he hugged her and kissed her long and hard.

It was a warm, comfortable, familiar kiss, not on the level of heat that Luca could generate. But not unwelcome either. When he hugged her it seemed somehow insubstantial, like something was missing, not like the memory of being wrapped in Luca's bear hug.

"We have a lot to make up for," Charles said.

"How long have you been waiting here?"

"I got here this morning, went to your office and you weren't there, so I left my luggage with Gerda and did all the touristy stuff. This is a great city."

"I've been trying to tell you that. But before we catch up, I need to eat. I'm starving."

Hadley unlocked the door, and Charles followed her into her apartment. She turned on the lights and led him out to the balcony.

"What a view."

"Yes, I got lucky with this apartment. It overlooks the Arno River."

"Look, the bridge is all lit up. Cool."

"Yes, you can see the Ponte Vecchio from here."

"Where should I put my bags?"

"Well, there's only one bedroom. You'll be sleeping out here in the living room, so drop it anywhere."

"The couch?" Charles frowned.

"Charles, I haven't seen you in a year. A lot has changed."

"Your mom told me about your Italian fling."

"Luca is more than a fling."

"I can understand how you'd feel that way after I refused to come over. But I was waiting for you to realize you'd made a mistake and come home."

Hadley rolled her eyes. "I didn't make a mistake, and I wasn't planning to come home, but—"

"You missed me."

"I miss home."

Charles stashed his suitcases behind the couch. "I'll be right out here if you change your mind."

"Let's get dinner," Hadley suggested. "There's a great little trattoria around the corner."

"Do they have steak here?"

"Yes, they have a Bistecca alla Fiorentina, a large T-bone served blood rare."

"My kind of food."

"But you're in Italy, so I would suggest the pasta."

"I'll try some of yours. You always like to share. Lead the way." Was he being petty, implying that he was sharing her with another man?

He followed her out the door. As she locked up, Charles grabbed her hand, and they walked in tandem down the quiet cobblestone street. Hadley looked around nostalgically, imagining all the things she would miss about Florence if she left now.

They got to the restaurant, and the woman at the door led them to the back to a private table with a spectacular view of the river. She handed them each a menu.

Hadley ordered a bottle of Moscato and some appetizers. Fresh bread and a plate of olive oil was delivered to the table.

"This is one of our, I mean, one of my favorites.

Why don't you let me order for you. I'll get you the steak, and I'll get some seafood and pasta."

"I'm in your hands."

Hadley felt comfortable ordering in Italian since Charles had no idea how she was butchering the language. Typically, she let Luca do the ordering.

The food was delicious.

"I could get used to this," Charles raved. "I can see why you like it here."

"Could you really see yourself living here?"

"What kind of job could I get?"

"Riding a bus, counting passengers?" Hadley suggested. That was mean. But she had been trying to get her boyfriend to visit, practically begging him for the past year, until she had finally given up, and then she'd met Luca.

"You heard about that?"

"Yes, how do you think it made me feel to find out from my best friend that my boyfriend, who I thought was in law school, was counting passengers on the campus bus?"

"Are you disappointed?"

"Charles, I don't care what you do, I just want you to be happy. But I wish you had been honest with me."

"I thought you'd leave me. I didn't like law school. I missed you, and I couldn't focus."

"I hope you're not blaming me."

"If you had been there, I wouldn't have dropped out."

"So what have you decided to do?'

"I'm getting a master's degree in economics."

"That sounds promising."

"Yes, I'm enjoying it."

As the server brought out the meal, Charles started the inquisition.

"So tell me about your Italian lover."

Hadley groaned. This was not a conversation she relished having in public.

"He's a member of the Carabinieri, the Italian paramilitary police."

"So you fell for a guy in uniform."

Hadley had to admit Luca looked sexy in his uniform. That was indeed part of the allure.

"And is he?"

"Is he what?"

"Your lover?"

Hadley inhaled. "Can you honestly tell me you haven't slept with anyone since I left?" *And don't lie, I have eyes and ears all over that campus.* And she had her suspicions about her "best friend," whom she imagined was being very accommodating.

Charles looked sheepish.

"That's what I thought."

"I asked you not to go, and you left me anyway."

"I wanted to experience living in another country."

"Well, I let you go for six months, and then you didn't come home."

"You let me go? I decided to go, and I got a job in my major. Those jobs are hard to come by. I was very fortunate."

"Were you ever coming home?"

It had been an Italian standoff. She didn't want to leave Italy, and he refused to visit her. When she left, they'd argued and agreed that they were each free to date others, but she hadn't been serious about anyone until the accident, which was when she met Luca.

"I was lonely for a long time, but when you wouldn't even come over summer break, not even for two weeks, I moved on."

"With Luca."

"With Luca. And besides, he's not even in the picture anymore."

"Since when?"

"Since our trip to Venice."

"You went to Venice with him?"

"It was business."

"And you just broke up?"

"Maybe, I don't know. But why did you come here after all this time?"

"Because your mother was worried about you. And when she told me you had an Italian boyfriend..."

"You got jealous."

"We've been dating since we were freshmen. I thought..."

"That's what I thought too, but you never made a commitment, so I felt free to go to Italy."

Then Charles did something unexpected. He got down on one knee and presented her with a small velvet box.

"What is this?"

"Open it and see."

Hadley frowned. She opened the box and was greeted with a sizeable diamond in an antique setting that twinkled under the lights.

"It-it's beautiful," she had to admit. "Really beautiful."

"So will you marry me?"

The other restaurant patrons suddenly turned toward them expectantly.

"Charles, this is out of the blue. I can't give you an answer now. I have to think about it. What does this mean? Are you ready to move to Florence?"

"Not if we get married. You'll move back to the States."

"And what will I do there?"

"They have museums in America, don't they?"

"You sound like my mother. Do you even love me?"

"Of course." Charles removed the ring from its box and held it out for her inspection. "Don't shut me down."

"Let's talk about this at home." Hadley put the ring back in the box and returned it to him for the time being.

The other diners groaned, looked disappointed, and went back to their food. They probably thought she was a bitch. Maybe she was.

When they got to her apartment, she turned on the lights. They were both a little drunk, and she was exhausted.

"Well, I'm going to bed. We'll talk about this in the morning."

"Hadley, I didn't come all the way over here to sleep on the couch. I miss you. I miss being with you."

Hadley swayed on her feet. She didn't even remember what it was like to be with Charles. But if she was ever going to commit to him, she may as well sleep with him to see if they were even still compatible. Did that make her a slut? She was too inebriated to care.

"Okay, but just for tonight," she agreed.

He removed the ring from the box in his jacket pocket.

"And wear this," Charles said.

"I'm not ready to make a commitment."

"Well, then, just while you're thinking about it. I

want to see how it looks on you."

Hadley caved. "Just this one night."

"And for the time I'm here."

Hadley shrugged and he slipped on the ring.

"Now we're engaged," Charles announced.

"Temporarily," Hadley countered.

Charles hugged her and hurried her into the bedroom. He removed her clothes and his and tossed them on the floor. This was beginning to feel familiar. He would satisfy her, and then they'd have sex, and then he'd fall asleep the minute his head hit the pillow. It was all over in a minute. One and done.

"That was great," he said, and true to form, or maybe it was due to jet lag, he nodded off.

With Charles, there was a little foreplay, and she had an orgasm but not during sex. When Luca entered her, she climaxed *while* he was inside her, making each thrust count. That had never happened with Charles in all the years they had been together. And when she fell asleep, spooned in Luca's arms, they remained cuddled up all night. King Charles was definitely *not* a cuddler.

With Charles, the act was rote. Perhaps it was because she and King Charles had been dating for four years and it was like she was part of an old married couple. Whereas with Luca, the experience was new and exciting. With Luca, she felt cherished, like they were really making love. He could communicate well enough in English, but she preferred to listen to him speak Italian.

But Luca was out of the picture. He had obviously made his choice. Isabella was beautiful. She would turn any man's head.

She fell asleep turned away from Charles. She was

restless and kept waking up. She was—less than satisfied.

The next morning, Charles was up ahead of her and had taken a run along the Arno. He brought her breakfast from a local café.

"What do you want to do today?" he asked.

"Well, I'm off of work this week, so do you want to go sightseeing?"

"Sure."

Should she tell him now that it wasn't going to work out between them? What would a few days of sightseeing prove? But he had come all this way. And he had bought her a ring.

Maybe after they were together for a few more days, they'd settle back into their old habit. But that was the problem. She didn't want to settle. Was she giving him a chance because she no longer had a chance with Luca?

Chapter Sixteen

She and Charles spent the next few days touring Italy on day trips from Florence. A grueling twelve-hour day trip to Cinque Terre, a wine-tasting experience and a cooking class in the Tuscan countryside, a trip to the Leaning Tower in Pisa. At night, they dined out at restaurants and talked. Hadley found that they didn't have much to say to each other, and when Charles intimated he wanted sex, she feigned exhaustion.

"Listen, I need to take care of something at the office tomorrow morning, so you can sleep late."

She wasn't even sure Charles had heard her. He had already dozed off.

When she'd asked Charles to come to Europe, she had planned a fabulous month of travel for the two of them during her summer break. When he didn't come, she went off with some friends. It was a missed experience they could never recover. It left a lingering bitter taste of regret in her heart.

She got dressed and walked to her office.

"So you're back," Gerda said.

"Not yet. Just checking in. Charles is leaving tomorrow. He has to get back to classes. Is the Signore in?"

"Still in Venice. I don't expect him back until next week. He's supervising the return of the paintings to Florence where you and he can properly catalog them before they're turned over to the authorities. How are you enjoying your vacation?"

Hadley thrust her left hand into the pocket of her sweater, but nothing got past Gerda.

"Wait, is that an engagement ring?"

She removed her hand, and Gerda grabbed it and examined the ring.

"Oh, this. I forgot to take it off."

"Are you engaged?"

"Not really. I'm planning to give it back to Charles before he leaves."

"The Poor Rachmanus. Where do things stand with Luca? He's stopped in, and he's been calling every day. I told him you were traveling with a friend. He insisted on knowing if it was a female friend or a male friend."

"What did you tell him?"

"As little as possible, but he suspects."

"I don't know why he came by. We're not together anymore."

"That's not how it seemed to me. He was very anxious to talk to you. Why did you come in this morning? You could have called."

"Mainly to get away from Charles and put off the uncomfortable talk we're going to have to have."

"What about Luca?"

"What about him?"

Gerda turned toward the office entrance. "Speaking of Luca, that good-looking devil is standing outside the door."

Hadley turned and started to run back into the Signore's office.

"Tell him I'm not here."

"He's already seen you, the Poor Rachmanus. Looks

like you're going to have another uncomfortable talk."

Luca stormed in. "Where have you been?" he demanded. "I've been calling you and you won't answer your cell phone. When I got back from the police station, you had left the villa to go back to Florence. Why didn't you wait for me?"

"Let's go into the Signore's office," Hadley suggested. She walked into Massimo's office. Luca followed and slammed the door.

Hadley turned on him. "You were occupied with Isabella. You didn't seem to care what happened to me. You were all about protecting her."

"She needed protection. Her brother was threatening to kill her. You didn't need protection. You can handle yourself."

Hadley pursed her lips. "It's obvious you prefer her. She's beautiful and helpless, two qualities you can't seem to resist."

"All I did was verify that Isabella's attack on her brother was self-defense. As soon as I got her to press charges against Matteo, I asked if she had a friend she could stay with, and Cara, she doesn't even have a single friend in the world. I couldn't just leave her there in that empty villa, the only home she's ever known and that she will probably lose. I had to get her settled into a battered woman's shelter. She and Matteo have a legal right to the villa, but that will most likely be overturned in the courts by Ingrid. Matteo will be locked up for a long time. Then I left her and came back to you as soon as I could, but you were gone. And when I got back to Florence, Gerda said you were traveling with a friend. A friend or a boyfriend?"

Luca caught the glint of the diamond on her ring

finger and grabbed her by the shoulders.

"Is that an engagement ring? Hadley, are you engaged?"

"Not exactly."

"What does that mean, not exactly?"

"Look, I'm sorry I never mentioned this before, but I had a boyfriend back home. We'd been dating for four years. He didn't want me to come to Florence, but I came anyway. He just flew in while we were in Venice. I had no idea he was coming. I couldn't just leave him here alone."

"But you could leave me alone? So you got engaged?"

"He proposed and wanted me to try on the ring."

"I thought that we…"

"Luca, I can't spend my life looking over my shoulder at every pretty girl that catches your eye or that you want to rescue. Worrying that I'm somehow not enough. You can't help yourself. That's the Italian way."

"That's not my way," he said angrily. "Cara, you are being ridiculous. I only have eyes for you. How can you not know that I love you? Haven't I shown you how I feel in every way?"

"You never actually said the words," Hadley said stubbornly.

"What good is saying the words if you don't trust me? Where is the boyfriend now?"

"At my apartment."

"And have you slept with him?"

Hadley frowned but didn't respond.

"I guess I have my answer, then. Goodbye, Hadley." With Luca, it was always open and shut, black and white, right and wrong. He turned on his heels, opened the door, and rushed out into the Florence sunshine.

Tears pooled in her eyes. She should have stopped him. But she had betrayed him. She had only herself to blame. She walked out to Gerda's desk.

"Go after him," Gerda urged, handing Hadley a tissue.

"It's too late."

"It's never too late." After a brief silence, Gerda asked, "What are you going to do?"

"Go home." Did she mean home, as in home, back to Florida? Or home to her apartment to a man she was no longer in love with? As she wandered the streets of her adopted city, Hadley realized she was already home.

Chapter Seventeen

Hadley walked into her apartment. Charles was out on the balcony, enjoying the view.

"I'll miss this place when I'm gone," Charles said, "but we can come back on our honeymoon, do the European tour thing like you wanted."

"I wish you had come sooner." Hadley sighed. Before she had met Luca.

"Well, I'm here now. So did you give your notice?"

"Give my notice?"

"Yes, I thought that's why you were going in to the office. You need to start packing if we're going to make the flight tomorrow."

"What flight?" said Hadley, puzzled.

"I booked you a ticket on my flight so we could fly home together and announce the good news."

Hadley shook her head. "What gave you the idea I was going home?"

"You're still wearing my ring. You said you missed home. I just thought—"

This was worse than she'd thought.

Hadley removed the ring from her left hand and closed her right fist around it.

"Charles," she began. "I love my job. And now, more than ever, some exciting things are starting to happen. We found a cache of stolen art looted by the Nazis, and we're about to announce it to the world. The repercussions will be monumental."

"What does that have to do with us?"

"It has to do with me, Charles. I'm exactly where I want to be, doing exactly what I want to do."

"Playing around with a bunch of ancient paintings?"

"They're not ancient, they're from the Renaissance period—the fourteenth to the seventeenth century, to be exact."

Charles frowned. "I don't care what century they're from. We're getting married, so you need to come home and forget about your job. All you do is look at pictures."

"Is that what you think I do?"

"You can do that anywhere. You can always get another job."

"In Tallahassee, Florida?"

"Sure, they have the Museum of Florida History and the Antique Car Museum and the Florida Historic Capital Museum—"

"Charles, are you listening to yourself? I'm an art history major. There's no better place on earth for me than Florence, Italy. This city has everything I want and need."

"But I'm not here."

That about summed it up. Hadley walked out on the balcony and sat beside Charles. She opened his hand, placed the ring in it, then closed it gently around the stone.

"What are you doing?"

"This isn't going to work."

"Is this about Luca? I forgave you for that."

Hadley was losing patience.

"I did nothing to be forgiven for. We were on a break, and we both had agreed to date other people. I didn't go looking for anyone. It just happened. And anyway, we're not together anymore. I just broke up with him."

"Well, then, why can't you be with me?"

"Charles, we haven't seen each other in a year. We've grown apart. We're not the same people anymore. I want a career, *this* career in *this* city. I don't want to sit at home in Tallahassee, Florida, and regret not staying here for the rest of my life."

"I thought you loved me."

"I did love you. But I don't feel that way anymore. I'm sorry."

"What do you want me to do? Quit school, come and live over here, and do nothing?"

"Exactly. You do understand. You don't want to give up the things you love, and neither do I."

Charles's face crumpled. "You can't give us another chance?"

"The bottom line is that I don't want to marry you."

As the truth started to sink in, Charles became angry, pocketed the ring, and stood up abruptly.

"I'll go pack my things and stay at a hotel tonight, unless I can catch an earlier flight."

"You don't have to do that. We're friends. You're welcome to stay here."

Charles scowled. "I don't want to be just friends with you, Hadley. I asked you to marry me."

"And I'm flattered. Last year, before I left, I would have been over the moon if you had proposed. I wouldn't have gone overseas. But you didn't ask. You couldn't make a commitment, and you wouldn't even take off a few weeks to visit me. In hindsight, if we had gotten married, it wouldn't have worked out. We don't want the same things."

"How do you know that?"

Hadley exhaled. She hadn't wanted to hurt Charles's feelings. But she knew her own mind.

"Because now I know what real love is. I tossed it away, but I won't settle for anything less." There, she'd finally given voice to her true feelings. She was in love with Luca Ferrari. Despite the language barrier, despite the cultural barrier, she felt more at home in Italy with Luca than she ever did with King Charles. For all the good that would do her now.

Sulking, Charles strode into the bedroom and began slamming doors and drawers.

Jeesh, Hadley thought. *That was a close call*. King Charles had become a *royal* pain in the ass. It was past time to depose the monarch and send him back to America.

Chapter Eighteen

After King Charles left, Hadley threw herself into her work with a frenzy, putting in long hours, nights, and weekends. That left no time to think about Luca and imagining what he and Isabella were up to.

She and Massimo went over to the storage unit every day to catalog the looted works, held meetings with government agencies, museum representatives, and others who could help them trace the provenance of the paintings so they could be returned to their proper owners. Some victims of the Holocaust were no longer alive and had no heirs. That represented a different set of challenges.

Hadley had been deposed by attorneys in the *Amore* case and had turned over Karrissa's diary to Ingrid's lawyer. She and Isabella, who had authenticated the diary and had also provided the records her grandfather had kept and the paperwork Matteo had kept documenting the sale of the paintings, had testified remotely in a court case. She hadn't spoken to Isabella since the trip to Venice. If she and Luca were together now, she didn't want to know.

She had to admit that Isabella did need protection from someone. She had probably been abused by her brother throughout her young life or at the very least terrorized since her mother had died. On top of that, she was most likely going to lose her home. She had no friends, to speak of. Matteo was her only contact with the outside world, and he was truly a monster. And the fact that Luca had come to her rescue was one of the things she loved most about her former lover. If she couldn't get past the fact that Isabella was so beautiful, that was *her* problem, *her* insecurity. But given the choice, any man would have chosen Isabella. So that was that.

The German government had intervened, demanding that *Amore* be sent back to Berlin and housed in The Gemäldegalerie with the rest of the European masterpieces. It was an uphill battle but, in the end, justice was served.

The remainder of the looted art stored in the villa had to be dealt with, and that could take years to process.

One day Gerda shook her awake after she'd fallen asleep at her desk.

"Hadley, go home. Massimo is taking his wife out to lunch, and then he's taking the rest of the day off. He told me to tell you to leave early."

"But isn't it Friday?"

"Yes."

"Isn't he with whatever-her-name-is?"

"That affair is over. Massimo is devoted to his wife. He's too busy to cheat."

"It's about time."

"You've been working too hard. You need to go home, get an early start on the weekend. Have you heard anything from King Charles?"

Groggy, Hadley reached in the drawer and grabbed her purse. "Word on the street is he's engaged to my best friend. And he's given her the same ring he gave me."

"How do you feel about that?"

"Relieved. Now I don't have to feel guilty about

ruining his life. Frankly, I don't feel anything for him and even less for her."

"Well, go home and get some rest. And, oh, before you get there, could you do me a favor and cut across the park and stop by that little leather boutique on the corner? I ordered a gift for Massimo's wife, and I want to give it to Massimo when he comes in Monday. It's already paid for."

"Sure, and I'll see you bright and early Monday morning."

Chapter Nineteen

Hadley could hardly keep her eyes open. She was walking across the park toward the leather shop when a large dog jumped on her and knocked her down.

"What?" she said groggily until she recognized Bocelli.

"Oh, Bocelli." She sighed. "I've missed you." Bocelli licked her face and wouldn't let her move when she tried to get up.

"What are you doing off your leash? Where's your—"

Then she saw Luca in his uniform looming over her. He offered her a hand up. When his hand touched hers, she inhaled, and her heart skipped a beat.

"You look a little dizzy. Let's sit down on the bench there." As he led her over, Bocelli trotted faithfully behind.

She looked at Luca suspiciously. "What are you doing here?"

"Bocelli and I were just out for a walk."

"And you just happened to pick this park at this particular time? And you're wearing your uniform?"

"I just got off my shift and, well, Gerda might have told me you would be walking through."

So Gerda was in on it. And the leather store was just a ruse. Of course.

Luca inched toward her on the bench, and her

insides heated up. If he got any closer, she was going to faint on the spot. She wanted to jump into his arms and kiss him right here in this park, but she resisted the urge.

"I'd like to introduce myself. I'm Luca Ferrari, and this is my dog Bocelli."

Hadley laughed.

"Can we start over, Cara?" Luca asked softly. "I have missed you."

"What about Isabella?"

"I've checked up on her by telephone to make sure she's okay, but I haven't seen her since Venice. Matteo is behind bars. She's making good progress. What about Charles?"

"He left the day I saw you in my office. He's already engaged to someone else."

"Good to know."

Bocelli was sitting at heel in front of her, breathing heavily and slobbering.

"What is this?" Luca asked. "There seems to be a box tied around Bocelli's neck."

Hadley petted Bocelli and examined his neck. There was indeed a box with a bow, tied with a ribbon around the dog's neck.

"Let's have a look," Luca said, his voice low and throaty.

Luca untied the ribbon and handed Hadley the box.

"I think this is meant for you," he said. His hand slipped, and he almost dropped the box. He rubbed his palm through his hair and held out the gift.

"For me?"

"Yes, it's from Bocelli and me."

She nervously unwrapped the box and opened it.

"It's a ring!" she exclaimed, trying to still her racing

heart.

Luca got down on bended knee next to Bocelli and looked adoringly into Hadley's eyes. The park fell away, and she could see only him.

"Bocelli and I would like to marry you."

Bocelli barked and then howled.

Hadley laughed.

"We practiced that," Luca said with a serious face. "We've also been practicing "*Con Te Partirò*.""

"Time to Say Goodbye?"

"Yes, it was a very melancholy song, and it made us miss you more."

"Bocelli likes classical pop?"

"Of course. He's a very smart dog."

The problem with Luca and his dog were that they were so damn irresistible.

He took the ring out of the box and slipped it onto her finger. It was an exquisite, square-cut emerald flanked by two sizeable diamonds.

"Luca, this ring is gorgeous. But how can you afford—"

"Hush," he said, touching his warm fingers to her lips and began stringing together a torrent of tender words in Italian. Loving words. Healing words.

"It's a family heirloom, Cara," he whispered. "I want you to have it. You are my family. You are my heart."

For a moment she didn't have the words. A huge ache rose inside her, an ache that had been building since she and Luca parted, and tears spilled out and streamed down her face.

She took Luca's darling face in her hands and kissed him.

"Is that a yes?" he asked.

Hadley smiled and looked into her beloved's face.

"You know what they say—love the dog, love the man," Hadley answered.

"Do you?" he asked plaintively. "Love me?"

"With all my heart."

Luca rose, pulled her up from the bench, enfolded her in his arms, and began kissing her. Bocelli barked, and a crowd that had gathered around them cheered.

She was literally shaking, and so was Luca. It felt so good, so right, to be back in his arms.

"I need to have you alone," Luca said urgently.

"I happen to know an apartment nearby, with a great view of the Arno." She smiled.

"Lead the way!" He laughed, fastening Bocelli's leash on his collar and petting him, Bocelli's tail wagging furiously.

"Good job, boy. We got the girl." Luca took hold of Hadley's hand and held on like he never wanted to let go. "Mamma has been cooking all day. We're going to my parents' house tonight to celebrate."

"Were you so sure I would say yes?"

"I hoped."

"I thought your mother wanted you to marry a nice Italian girl."

"She did."

If Hadley knew anything, she knew it was never a good idea to stand between an Italian man and his mamma.

"My mamma has old-fashioned ideas. With Mamma, everything is always black or white. There are never any gray shades."

"I wonder who you take after," Hadley said under

her breath.

"I, on the other hand, am very flexible."

Hadley raised her brows. "I could pretend I'm Italian."

Luca laughed. "Cara, you speak Italian with a Southern accent."

"What if they don't like me?'

"They will love you because I love you. How could they not? And I've already booked the Duomo. So your parents and family can come over and witness our wedding." Hadley was a little nervous about telling her mother, but her mind was made up. She loved Luca and she was going to marry him, no matter what.

"You were very sure of me."

"I was sure I couldn't live without you."

Chapter Twenty

The phone wouldn't stop ringing. The Massimo Domingo Art Detective Agency was suddenly thrust into the spotlight. Newspaper reporters and broadcasters called to get the details about the lost masterpiece. Museum directors from around the world called to congratulate Massimo and to set up luncheon meetings and phone calls with the Signore. An array of new consultation cases flowed into the agency. They were going to have to staff up soon. It was much more than she and Gerda could handle. Massimo was pulling his weight now. Gone were the Friday afternoon trysts with his mistress. His wife was keeping a tight rein on him. She was happy to continue investing in what was now a going concern.

Signore Domingo's publisher called to tell Massimo his *Pocket Guide* had sold out and was on the second printing. And they contracted him for a second book. She had never seen the Signore so happy.

Ingrid could have made millions selling *Amore*, but she chose to loan it for an indefinite period to the Uffizi Gallery, where it would be displayed along with Botticelli's other two masterpieces. *Amore* had its own room around the corner from *Primavera* and *Birth of Venus*, with a special plaque in tribute to the Adelman family and a display featuring the family's history, complete with the old photos Ingrid provided.

Ingrid had consulted Hadley after she'd received dozens of lucrative offers from private parties, corporations, auction houses, and museums. Hadley made her feelings known. The world had gone for centuries without seeing *Amore*. Had Ingrid considered what joy and inspiration she could bring to museum visitors from around the world? She could maintain legal ownership of the work, and Uffizi donors had immediately raised funds to offer Ingrid for the loan of the painting and to fund a special exhibit of the paintings discovered in the villa while their rightful owners were being tracked down. The museum was eternally grateful to Hadley for her role in making this happen.

Ingrid decided to stay in Italy during the various trials and for the duration of the Uffizi exhibit of her family's paintings. She was finally awarded the deed to the villa, and she asked Isabella to move in with her while she was in Italy. When she left to return to her life in America, she granted Isabella permission to stay there for as long as she liked—forever, if she chose. She would help Isabella deal with Matteo whenever he was released from custody.

Hadley hung up the phone, shock still registered on her face.

"What happened?" Gerda asked, coming over to Hadley's desk.

"That was the director of the Uffizi. He offered me a job as assistant curator. My first assignment would be to curate the 'Lost Masterpieces' exhibit."

"That's wonderful. What did you tell him?"

"I told him I'd have to think it over."

"What's there to think about?" Gerda exclaimed. "That's your dream job."

"I still have a lot to learn here."

"Hadley, *you* tracked down that lost masterpiece and the other looted paintings. Not Massimo. And *you* deserve the credit."

"Maybe, but—"

"Maybe nothing. You march into Massimo's office and demand a raise if you plan to stay or tell him you're taking another job. The boss is in a good mood. He just gave me a big raise and a promotion."

"Well deserved, Gerda."

"Thank you."

Hadley stood in front of Gerda's desk so she couldn't get away.

"Now tell me what's wrong. Why do you keep taking off to go to the doctor?"

Gerda blushed.

"I wasn't really at the doctor's. I was *with* a doctor. I met him on that new Italian dating website."

"Really. Tell me."

"Well, you know I never thought I would find anyone after my Fritz passed. Especially at my age. There was never going to be another man for me. But then I met this doctor online. He lost his wife, and he's as lonely as I am. He's very sweet and considerate."

"You'd better be careful. There are some real weirdos out there."

"I had Massimo investigate him," Gerda said. "He passed with flying colors."

"Oh, Gerda, I'm so happy for you." Hadley noticed there was a sparkle in Gerda's eyes and a new spring in her step.

"Thank you. Now it's your turn for something good to happen."

Hadley knew Gerda was right, but she'd been working at the agency only six months. Who was she to demand anything? She'd been lucky to answer the phone when Ingrid called, but was she just in the right place at the right time, or was she instrumental in solving the case? And she wasn't proud of the way she had handled things—lying to Massimo from the very beginning.

Rising from her chair in the outer office, she gathered her courage and walked into Massimo's office. His door was open, and his legs were propped on his desk in a leisurely pose. In one hand was a glass of wine, in his other hand a pastry she'd brought to him this morning from the café around the corner.

"Signore Domingo—Massimo. I'd like to talk to you about something."

"Please, have a seat." Massimo welcomed her into his office. "I was just coming to talk to you. What's on your mind?"

"I just got a phone call from the director of the Uffizi Gallery, and they offered me the job of assistant curator. They're creating a new position for me. They want me to curate the 'Lost Masterpieces' exhibit."

Massimo rose from his desk, threw up his hands, and shouted, "Impossible! I won't allow it."

"It was an impressive offer."

"I'll match their salary," Massimo said, "and raise it."

"Signore, that's very generous."

"You deserve it. You singlehandedly breathed life into a dying agency. I feel like a new man. I feel ten years younger."

"I was only following the guidelines in your *Pocket Guide*."

"Very diplomatic of you to say, but your contribution was invaluable. And now I have more work than I can handle."

Hadley took a deep breath while weighing her options. On the one hand was her dream job at the Uffizi, at a significant raise in pay. On the other hand, Signore Domingo needed her. The cases pouring in were fascinating—tracking down paintings that had been missing for decades. Retrieving and returning personal property to deserving clients. Hot on the trail of missing masterpieces. An exciting prospect.

"Will the job involve running your errands?" Hadley ventured.

"That will not be a part of your new job description," Massimo replied confidently. "We're hiring a new employee who will be running *your* errands. You will be too busy with your additional responsibilities."

Massimo was right. Untangling the provenance of the cache of stolen art they had discovered in the Venetian villa would take larger firms than theirs a lifetime.

"But curating such a prestigious exhibit would be a once-in-a-lifetime opportunity," she pointed out.

"Of course, I will agree to *loan* you to the Uffizi for the duration of the exhibit. It will shine the light on our agency."

"*Our* agency?"

"Yes," said the Signore. "I'm prepared to give you a hefty raise, your own office, *and* your name on the letterhead."

Hadley hesitated. "Do we even have letterhead?"

"No, but we will. My wife insists. I owe a lot to that woman."

Massimo sat up straight in his chair and affected a more serious tone. "I took her for granted," he admitted. "I took you for granted. That will never happen again. I did things I wasn't proud of because it boosted my ego, made me feel more of a man. She wants me to cut back on the pasta, which I will do after I finish this delectable pastry you brought me."

Hadley doubted Massimo would make good on that particular promise, but she had high hopes about his fidelity.

"I've disappointed her for far too long. If she wants letterhead, she'll get letterhead. I gave her carte blanche in redecorating. She has big plans for your office."

It didn't take Hadley long to come to a decision.

"Well, I can hardly refuse, then. I'll stay."

"Wonderful." Massimo poured Hadley a glass of lightly sparkling sweet white wine, her favorite. "My wife sent this bottle of Moscato to help us celebrate. She's proud of what we've accomplished."

"Was she so sure I'd accept your offer?"

"Don't underestimate my wife. She's a very smart woman."

"I hope you'll remember that."

Massimo placed a decorative bag on his desk with Hadley's name on the gift tag. "Here's another bottle for you and young Luca."

"Thank you." Hadley drained her glass and picked up the gift bag.

"If it's okay with you, I'll be leaving early to celebrate in private with Luca. Isn't that Rule Number Ten of your *Pocket Guide*? Savor Your Successes?"

"Indeed. Meanwhile, Gerda and I will prioritize our caseload."

"I'll be in bright and early Monday morning to start making progress on our new projects."

"Get plenty of rest," Massimo added.

Hadley smiled and thought of the ways she and Luca would celebrate. Somehow, she didn't think she would be getting much sleep in the next few days.

Part Two
The Case of the Vanishing Vermeer

"Art evokes the mystery without which the world would not exist."

~René Magritte

"The Art of Vermeer must have been there on the morning of creation."

~Frederick Sommer

Chapter Twenty-One

Rule Number One: Think Twice before Drawing Conclusions. If something feels or appears right to you, trust your instincts. Don't second-guess yourself. Your first *impressionisms* (ha-ha) are usually on target.

~*Massimo Domingo's Pocket Guide to Stolen Art Recovery—Volume 2*

Hadley Evans swung her shapely, recently shaved legs up on her new mahogany desk, trying it on for size. In fact, the desk was supersized, courtesy of Signora Francesca Domingo, Massimo Domingo's long-suffering wife. Massimo had given Francesca carte blanche to redecorate the suite of offices, and she had gone to town, even out of town, to purchase everything she needed—from antique furniture and designer window treatments to handmade Italian floor tiles.

Signora Domingo had taken complete control of her husband's life at work and at home. She'd even signed Massimo up for a men's book club to keep him occupied in what little spare time he now had. Hadley and Gerda, Massimo's secretary and office manager, had discussed Massimo's book club just this morning.

"What kind of books do they read?" Hadley wondered.

"They're currently reading *A Man Called Ove*."

"Does every book have to have 'Man' in the title?"

"I don't think so," said Gerda. "They read mostly books about sports."

"That figures."

"She doesn't care what they read as long as it keeps him out of trouble."

"Do you think she knew about Massimo's string of mistresses?"

"I'm sure she did," asserted Gerda. "Everybody knew about them. But she seems to have forgiven him, and now he's too busy to cheat."

"Keeping him occupied seems to have cured his infidelity," agreed Hadley. "Talking about cures, how's the doctor, by the way?"

Since Gerda had started dating her internist, happiness shone brightly in her eyes and was reflected in the new spring in her step. After a long season without companionship, unflappable Gerda had finally been bitten by the love bug.

"He's fine. How about Officer Sexy?"

Hadley smiled her Mona Lisa smile. But she had no hidden secret. Her love for Luca was apparent for all to see.

"He's excited about the wedding."

"And what about you?"

Gerda knew Hadley too well. Well enough to sense her hesitation.

Examining her new Ferragamos®, which she could now afford on her increased salary, she realized her problem was more personal than work-related. She was getting cold feet.

Everything was going great with her job, with her new promotion, and the challenging work she was doing at the Massimo Domingo Art Detective Agency. The

Signore was back in all his glory. Art experts from around the world sought him out for consultation. He was the darling of the media. Phones were ringing, business was booming. There hadn't been much time for personal reflection.

"If you need any help with the plans, you know you can count on me, and Francesca would love to get involved. In fact, she would gladly take over the entire event."

Not that Hadley minded Signora Domingo's ever-looming presence at the office and in their lives. Surveying her large new quarters, she looked out onto Piazza della Signoria, teeming with tourists and townspeople alike. The public square was the gateway to the Uffizi Gallery, perhaps her favorite place in Florence, and Piazza del Duomo, which just reminded Hadley of her upcoming nuptials.

Il Duomo, recognizable above the terracotta rooftops of Florence from anywhere in the city, loomed large in the distance and in her mind. She was scheduled to get married there in a few short months. And she hadn't even made a dent in winning over Luca's mother. The woman was insistent that her son marry a nice Italian girl. Hadley spoke passable Italian, but with an American Southern accent. Luca had tried to introduce her as a girl from Sicily—the Deep South of Italy. But that ploy hadn't worked.

"You speak Italian like a child, Cara," Luca observed.

"So you've said. I'm taking Italian lessons."

Then he recommended she praise his mother's red sauce.

"Tell her it is the best spaghetti sauce you've ever

tasted." Mama Ferrari saw right through that. Flattery was getting Hadley nowhere. She couldn't change who she was.

"You will impress my mother if you can learn to cook like an Italian."

"Then I'll sign up for a cooking class," Hadley replied, pursing her lips. *Italian men and their mothers.* That was a phenomenon she would have to come to grips with. "That's two strikes against me. Why are you looking to change me? I thought you loved me the way I am."

"Of course, I do, Cara. My mother will warm up to you as soon as we start having some bambinos."

"*Some* bambinos?"

"Yes, it will be very merry."

"What do you mean?"

"Isn't that how you say it in America?"

Hadley wore a puzzled expression.

"More is merrier," Luca said.

"The more the merrier?"

"Si."

Hadley blew out a breath. Now was not the time to have this argument. She was wearing Luca's engagement ring. She loved her fiancé, but she could tell she would have some tough decisions ahead. A houseful of bambinos or a career. Marriage was all about compromise.

Hadley frowned. Conversely, her parents were less than thrilled with her choice of husbands. To Hadley, Luca Ferrari was the whole package. Tall, handsome, good-natured, sweet, and sexy, if not a bit overprotective. But their idea of the perfect son-in-law was King Charles, her longtime boyfriend, whose proposal she had recently spurned. They were constantly haranguing her to return to Tallahassee, Florida, and marry a successful attorney or a corporate CEO or an up-and-coming politician, anyone who wasn't a police detective or who lived on a police detective's salary and who didn't live an ocean away. Someone who belonged to the right country club. Did they even have country clubs in Italy?

Never mind that King Charles had moved on with Hadley's best "frenemy." Her parents dropped the hint that he was always asking about Hadley whenever they got together with Charles's parents. They intimated that Charles would be happy to forgive her and give her another chance. He'd cheated on her before and now he was ready to cheat again. Once a cheater…

Apparently, her feelings for Luca didn't enter into her parent's equation. They wondered how well she knew him. In truth, she had just met him last year while attending a college abroad program in Italy and had decided to stay in Florence to work for Massimo Domingo as a junior art detective. She would have taken a job as a street sweeper to stay in the city and pursue her career in art history. Luca was just icing on the cake. But maybe she *was* rushing into the relationship.

She'd dated other men besides Luca in Florence. One, the son of a colonel on the nearby Army base in Pisa, had broad appeal for the weekly barbecues held on the base. After months of eating nothing but pasta and pizza, she would have done almost anything for a hamburger. There were other indiscretions. Too much sambuca may have played a role, she recalled. But, in the end, her heart had won out over her stomach and she'd fallen in love with Luca Ferrari, the Carabiniere who had arrested her for walking in the street and getting run over by a motorcyclist when she first arrived in Florence. Her beat cop had since become a full-fledged detective. They had that in common. They were both in the business of solving crimes.

A single bell chimed from Giotto's Bell Tower, tolling the suspension of work for the lunch break at 11:30 a.m. Every day bells rang singly at 7 a.m., noon, and at sunset indicating "Angelus," reminding Hadley that the clock was ticking and time was running out. She needed to kick herself into gear, stop wallowing in relationship self-doubt, and start making progress in contacting the families of the Holocaust survivors to reunite them with the artwork she and Luca had recovered in the villa in Venice. Hadley's idea for the Uffizi to display the stolen works of art in a special exhibition had paid dividends. Because of the publicity, dozens of paintings were returned to the heirs of their original owners. But many more remained unclaimed in a rented warehouse in Florence.

She had no spare time to obsess over her wedding and whether or not she was making the right decision. She had important work to do. No time for second thoughts.

She picked up the latest edition of *Massimo Domingo's Pocket Guide to Stolen Art Recovery— Volume 2*. Maybe there were some lessons she could learn from Massimo's lifetime of experience.

Rule Number One: Think Twice Before Drawing Conclusions. If something feels or appears right to you, trust your instincts. Don't second-guess yourself. Your first *impressionisms* (ha ha) are usually on target.

Chapter Twenty-Two

Rule Number Two: Put Things In Perspective. Clarify the true value and assess the significance of each clue before making a final move.

~Massimo Domingo's Pocket Guide to Stolen Art Recovery—Volume 2

"How would you like to take a trip?" Massimo asked, interrupting her daydreaming.

Flustered, Hadley removed her legs from the desk and sat up straight in her new ergonomic office chair. "I'm always up for an adventure," she replied. "Where to?"

"Bellagio, on Lake Como."

Hadley's heart raced, and her eyes sparkled. Lake Como was one of her favorite destinations.

"What's in Lake Como?"

"The son of an old acquaintance of mine, an art dealer in Milan, called yesterday. Bruno Lombardi. He has a client, a Prince Alessandro Rossi, who was cleaning out his deceased parents' villa on the lake before getting it ready for sale when he discovered a painting he was unfamiliar with."

"What kind of painting?"

"He claims it's a Vermeer, of all things—*Woman in Pearls and a Red Dress.*"

"In Italy?"

"Apparently," Massimo stated, "although the client has no records, no provenance, no papers that would explain why his parents would own a Vermeer. There was no mention of a Vermeer in the will. He's not even sure it's an original. It's unlikely. You know Vermeer is one of the most widely forged artists. He produced less than fifty paintings, and only thirty-four paintings that survived are universally attributed to him."

Hadley had studied Vermeer in college. The artist worked slowly, producing about three paintings a year.

"But there are possibly another six lost works, at least," Massimo added, piquing Hadley's interest. "So, if there's a chance, however slight, Signore Lombardi would like us to authenticate it."

"Can't he just pack it up and mail it?"

"Hadley, if it's a real Vermeer, we can't take that chance. It could be priceless. Or it could be a worthless fake. I don't have the time to spare. I'm doing a television special on stolen Nazi art. They're filming it at the Uffizi tomorrow. But we need to move on this."

"Imagine if it is authentic, what a coup that would be," Hadley said.

"Odds are this is another fake," Massimo said, shaking his head. "And I don't completely trust this dealer."

"Didn't you say you were friends?"

"*Acquaintances*. Lately, everyone is a friend. He wouldn't give me the time of day for years. You know a lot of art dealers were complicit in the German scheme to pressure Jews into selling their valuables in order to survive the war. Now their firms have become 'respectable.' But the things that were done during the war, you can't even imagine."

"I'll take that into consideration," Hadley agreed. "I'd love to go back to Lake Como. Thank you for trusting me with this assignment."

"Okay, tell Gerda to book you at the Grand Hotel Villa Serbelloni." He handed her a thick envelope. "The particulars are inside, including Signore Lombardi's contact information, his gallery and home address, the client's name, and the address of the villa. I want you to go to the villa, find out as much as possible from the client about this painting, check out the condition of the work and, if the client is willing, bring it back to me in Florence."

"Do we know the size of the piece?"

"Small format as usual—17½ x 15 inches, oil on canvas. Small enough for you to easily bring it home on the train."

"Are there claims out on any Vermeers?"

"Not that I'm aware of. You'll need to do the research to track that down. Find out if it has ever been displayed in a museum or owned by any other private parties."

"Would you mind if I asked Luca to come?"

Massimo stroked his chin. "I don't anticipate any trouble. Why would you need a Carabiniere along?"

Other than a chance to go to the most romantic location in Italy with her fiancé? "He was a lot of help in Venice," Hadley pointed out. "Without Luca, that whole case could have gone down differently."

Massimo hesitated. "True, okay, it couldn't hurt. But I'm not paying for an extra room."

That won't be necessary," Hadley said, smiling. She and Luca were sleeping together. Surely the Signore would know that. Why would they need a separate room?

"The shortest way is to drive, just under four hours, or you could take a train."

"Yes, sir."

As soon as Massimo left her office, Hadley took the envelope and walked over to Gerda's desk.

"I hear some lucky person is going to Bellagio."

"You heard correctly. I can't wait. I'm going to see if Luca can get some time off and come with me."

"A pre-honeymoon?"

Hadley blushed. That would certainly be a perk.

After she called Luca to see if he could arrange some days off, Hadley did some preliminary research about the Dutch Master. Auction records suggested that Johannes Vermeer painted a number of unattributed or lost works: a self-portrait, a painting of a man washing his hands, a street scene, a *Visit to the Tomb*, a mythological painting of Jupiter, and an early painting known as "a face by Vermeer." Or what she was going to see could be an entirely unidentified work by the master, unknown in previous documents. But what was it doing in a villa in Italy, and how had that vanishing act happened?

Although he was an avid art collector and dealer, Vermeer never went abroad. She would follow the Signore's lead and look for clues. There must be a record of the painting somewhere. If it was appropriated by the Germans, she could find it. Germans were mad about keeping records. And she would remain cautious about the art dealer and his motives. Trust but verify was the best course of action.

Over the years, Vermeers had been stolen. Could the piece in question have been stolen, resold, and kept from public view all these years? Hoarded away in the vault of a private collector, an art afficionado, away from

149

prying eyes? If she could find a genuine Vermeer previously thought destroyed or lost to public view, the art world would stand up and take notice. Could she recognize an authentic Vermeer or spot an imitation? Tracking down the provenance would be challenging, but that's what she was trained to do. And Massimo was depending on her.

Vermeer's remarkable trademark use of a pearly light might help identify the piece. Or his signature color palette of blues, yellows, and grays. Almost all his paintings were of contemporary subjects, domestic interiors set in two rooms in his house in Delft, mostly women, often the same people, lit by a window on the left. As far as she knew, he'd only dated three of his paintings.

There was no photo of the artwork in the envelope. Coming face to face with a Vermeer would be thrilling and worth the trip alone. Of course, she had studied the artist's works extensively, and she had seen Vermeers in various museums: The Rijksmuseum in Amsterdam and the Metropolitan Museum of Art in New York, and her favorite of his masterpieces, *Girl with a Pearl Earring*, the summer of 2013 when it was on loan from The Frick Collection in New York to the High Museum of Art in Atlanta, in the Masterpieces from the Royal Picture Gallery.

She had to admit, she was unfamiliar with this particular painting. He painted *Girl with a Red Hat*, and there was a beautiful red gown featured in *Girl with a Wine Glass*. Could it be an earlier version of *Girl with a Pearl Earring*? Many artists painted the same scene over and over, at different times of day in different lights, or used the same muse or subject in all of their paintings.

Pearls appeared in eight paintings by Vermeer. But this painting could be unique.

The chance to see a relatively unknown Vermeer up close and personal and visit magical Lake Como was an irresistible opportunity. Not to mention the added bonus of spending time with Luca.

Chapter Twenty-Three

Rule Number Three: Don't Get Bogged Down In The Visible Details Of Realism. Sometimes you can get too close to a problem and doubt what you're looking at.
~Massimo Domingo's Pocket Guide to Stolen Art Recovery—Volume 2

Massimo sprang for a private car—a Mercedes E class premium service—to pick Hadley and Luca up from the train station in Milan and transport them to the Grand Hotel Villa Serbelloni in Bellagio. It was a smooth but twisty drive with breathtaking scenery all along the way. The car deposited them and their luggage directly in front of the hotel, and the porter came out and took their bags. The view from outside the hotel was magnificent.

"Welcome to the Grand Hotel Villa Serbelloni," stated the man as he ushered them inside. Hadley had been to Lake Como, but never to Bellagio. She and her family had stayed at a less expensive hotel in Menaggio, a little way down the lake.

Hadley refreshed the facts she'd discovered about Vermeer on the train. An innkeeper, running the family business, he was a Dutch Golden Age Baroque Period painter, an art dealer, and an avid art collector, but he died in debt. His wife gave birth to fifteen children—four of them were buried before being baptized.

It was likely the painting had been originally owned by Peter van Ruijven, Vermeer's patron who owned many of his works, purchased directly from the artist, passed on to his family, who had likely auctioned off part of his collections to private owners.

An unknown collector had probably plucked the painting from oblivion and sold it to some wealthy patron, perhaps a royal. She'd need to do some digging to see if any museums, like the Rijksmuseum, had acquired it at any point in time. Had it appeared in any exhibitions? But what was the Italian connection? What was the painting's fate during World War II? Had it fallen into the hands of the Nazis or Mussolini? The Milanese art collector had a sketchy reputation, but his son was now running the business. Was he of the same ilk as his father? Was he aware of how his father had conducted business during the war? Was he as shady as his father had been, or was his whitewashed reputation as stellar as it appeared to be? Had he inherited his father's collection? Were they on display in his gallery or hidden away so no one could appreciate them?

To date, Hadley had been able to determine the following facts about the provenance of *Woman in Pearls and a Red Dress*. Her notebook stated:

Woman in Pearls and a Red Dress

c. 1664 oil on canvas 44/5 cm x 39 cm (17.5 in. x 15 in.)

(?) Pieter Claesz. van Ruijven, Delft (d. 1674); (?) his widow, Maria de Knuijt, Delft (d. 1681);

(?) their daughter, Magdalena van Ruijven, Delft (d. 1682);

(?) her widower, Jacob Abrahamsz Dissius (d. 1695);

Dissius sale, Amsterdam, 16 May, 1696.

Unidentified London sale (Christie's), 10 May, 1861.

Collection Bellisario Family, Venice c. 1884, antiques dealer, sold to a private party and bought back.

Prince Fritz Hohenstaufen, Villa di Mare, Venice.

Anonymous third-party sale.

The latter dates of purchase were unlisted. The painting had been scheduled for display January 25-April 28, 1928, in Rome at the Galleria Borghese, along with *Girl with a Pearl Earring* and *The Love Letter*, during the rule of Benito Mussolini, the Fascist dictator of Italy from 1925 to 1945. But it never made it to the exhibition, and all traces of the masterpiece had since disappeared. Mussolini aligned himself with Adolf Hitler, a voracious "art collector," so it didn't pay to ask too many questions. That hardly surprised Hadley. Some twenty percent of the art in Europe was looted by the Nazis and well over 100,000 items had still not been returned to their rightful owners.

It was not the first time a Vermeer had gone missing. Hadley knew that Signore Domingo would give anything to locate an authentic Vermeer. He'd had a role in trying to track down Vermeer's *The Concert*, which was part of a large art heist that took place in March 1990 at the Isabella Stewart Gardner Museum when a group of thieves entered the museum dressed as Boston police. They stole thirteen paintings, including Vermeer's masterpiece. Signore Domingo considered the fact that the paintings were still missing one of his greatest failures. When he was unable to recover the treasures, his reputation had spiraled downward.

That same elusive painting had quite a checkered

history. It had been sold in Amsterdam in 1696 and did not resurface for more than a hundred years. It was purchased by Isabella Stewart Gardner in 1892 in Paris for $5,000. Now valued at an estimated $200 million, it held the record for the most valuable unrecovered artwork in the world. Who knew what *Woman in Pearls and a Red Dress* would be worth today?

"Why do you care about tracing the provenance of a painting?" Luca wondered when they were settled in their hotel room.

"Because it provides evidence of its origin," explained Hadley. "A painting's history can be established by verifying the chain of custody. Who owned the painting, where it was stored, and whether it was part of an exhibition."

"So you are a detective, like me?" Luca asked.

"Exactly," said Hadley.

In order to establish provenance and help authenticate the artwork, Hadley began checking auction records. The odds were against her. She knew establishing an unbroken line of provenance of older paintings was rarely achieved. She'd feverishly consulted the requisite websites. Her fingers flew over the computer keys. The IFAR (International Foundation for Art Research) site yielded nothing. The *Essential Vermeer Interactive Catalogue* listed no auction records for this particular painting. Any details on the painting— style, subject, size of the work, and its description, signature, materials, dimensions, and frame—were nonexistent or, at best, sketchy. Records of sale from the more distant past didn't often survive. And records could be forged or destroyed for dubious reasons. The titles of paintings and the attribution to a particular artist frequently change over time. Many private collectors buy and sell works anonymously through third parties, art dealers or auction houses, which may or may not disclose the owner's identity, even that of art thieves.

"Is a painting with a good provenance more valuable than one without it?" Luca asked.

"Yes, because it is less likely to be a forgery or the work of an imitator. However, provenance alone is not enough to establish the authenticity of a painting, especially if it is considered of value."

Luca looked out the hotel window at the sparkling lake and mountain vista and breathed a heavy sigh. "This must be the most beautiful place on earth."

"I agree. Wouldn't it be great to live here year 'round?"

"It would be expensive," Luca pointed out.

"How would you make a living? I doubt if much crime goes on at the lake."

"You'd be surprised, Cara. You know the TV shows about those quiet English villages where a murder happens every week and serial killers lurk behind every garden gate?"

"True. But what would I do?"

"You'd be married to me and spend your life making me happy and raising our babies."

"Dream on. I guess I could have an affair with a fabulous actor with a home on the lake."

"You forget, Cara, I'm carrying a gun, and I would have to challenge your lover to a duel."

"You brought your gun?" Hadley frowned.

"It came in handy in Venice. You never know what dangers lurk on the lake."

"I think you see danger around every corner."

Luca's expression turned serious. "That's my job, Hadley. To protect the innocent."

"Well, in this case, we're protecting a work of art."

"According to you, a very *valuable* piece of art. In my experience, where money is involved, men tend to stretch the limits of the law. And sometimes seeking justice requires taking risks."

"You may be right. Men have done some serious things for the sake of art."

Luca turned toward the lake. "When can we get out on the water?"

"Right after lunch. We'll hire a boat to take us to Villa Rossi."

"First things first, Cara. I need a workout. My body needs to stretch after all that time on the train and in the car."

Hadley looked around the room. "I don't see any exercise equipment. I'm sure they have a gym in the hotel."

Luca took her hand and led her over to the king-sized bed. "That's not the kind of workout I had in mind."

Hadley blushed.

****

After their "exercise" session, Hadley and Luca enjoyed a nice lunch outside by the pool with an iconic view of the majestic lake and mountains to pass the time before their appointment.

"I could get used to this," Luca said, shielding his eyes from the sun.

"Don't get too comfortable. We have a job to do, and we must be dedicated to doing it."

Luca looked into Hadley's eyes and tilted her chin

in his hand. "You are dedicated to me, no? And to raising our family?"

"Certo," replied Hadley. "But from now on, let's save the romance for after we finish this case." Sometimes she got the feeling Luca would like to remake her into his mother. A plump but attractive Italian woman who stayed at home, cooked pasta, and raised bambinos. The subject of bambinos hadn't even come up yet, until now. She was in love with Luca, but would she go as far as to say she was "devoted"? She knew she wouldn't give up her career for him. She did love pasta, even though she didn't know how to cook, and babies were cute, but she didn't intend to lose her figure right away.

"We can make time for both, Cara."

Luca tried to pay the bill, but Hadley tapped his wrist and signaled to the waiter to charge the meal to their room. It was business, after all. Luca thanked her, took her hand, and they walked out of the hotel toward the dock to catch the boat to Villa Rossi.

Being out on the lake on such a glorious day was invigorating. Hadley loved the water. The lake sparkled in the sun and changed colors, sometimes blue, sometimes green. The charter boat gently swayed as it glided peacefully across the lake and down some thirty-four kilometers to an exclusive area of villas in Cernobbio. The vessel pulled into a private boat dock, and Luca helped Hadley out.

"We'll call when we're ready to leave," Hadley told the captain.

"It's only a stone's throw away from Como, if you want to take in some sightseeing on the way back. And it's located in front of the Grand Hotel Villa d'Este.

That's worth a look."

"We'll let you know."

Approaching the property from the waterfront, Hadley's jaw dropped.

"It's heavenly," she breathed, taking in the perfectly manicured lawn, the stone steps, the landscaping—a lush garden with olive and lemon trees—and the sumptuous mansion itself, with balconies off each of what looked like four lakefront bedrooms in the three-story stone structure. On the side facing the lake was a large patio with a pool.

When they knocked on the door, Prince Alessandro Rossi introduced himself and welcomed them. She was expecting a butler. She'd never met a prince before and wondered if she should call him Your Highness or bow.

"Prince Alessandro, I'm Hadley Evans, and this is my associate, Luca Ferrari."

"Please, I don't stand on formality. Call me Sandro. It's very nice to meet you," he said. "May I offer you some refreshment? Some prosecco and biscotti, perhaps?"

"That would be lovely," Hadley said.

They sat on a comfortable flowered sofa in front of a fireplace. Off to the side was a spacious dining room with a crystal chandelier, and she caught a glimpse of a professional chef-worthy kitchen.

There was an elegant staircase rising to the second floor.

"You have a lovely home," Hadley said.

"Thank you. It belonged to my parents. I spent many memorable vacations here. It was built in the early 1900s," the prince noted, "but it has every modern convenience."

"Why would you ever want to leave?" Luca asked.

"You can imagine, with the taxes and upkeep, the costs are prohibitive. I also maintain a home in Rome, where my business is, so I'm afraid I have to give this up, although I will miss it." The prince rose from the couch. "Well, do you want to see her?"

"Her?" Luca asked.

"*The Woman in Pearls and a Red Dress*."

"Yes, of course," Hadley said. "Lead the way."

"I have her on display in the solarium so you can see her in just the right light."

"He talks of the woman in the painting like she's alive," Luca whispered, scratching his head.

"Luca, that is the way a patron thinks when they own a masterpiece. When you see her, you'll understand, if she was really painted by the Master. If she is indeed real, she will come alive before your eyes."

The prince led them into a sunlit solarium and stood transfixed in front of the painting.

Hadley drew a breath. If she thought the villa was breathtaking, the painting, and it *was* real, she was convinced, was even more magnificent.

While Hadley studied the painting, Prince Alessandro looked over his shoulder. Luca excused himself, saying he had to answer the call of nature. But instead of heading for the bathroom, he began to do some digging of his own around the comfortably appointed villa. He opened drawers and cabinets in all the rooms of the house and conducted a thorough search as if he'd had a warrant, which he definitely didn't have. But who knew if they'd have another opportunity to explore the premises again. People tended to get uncooperative, especially when something was at stake as valuable as this painting apparently was.

The prince turned to Hadley. "Well, what do you think?"

"I'm speechless," Hadley admitted.

"It is authentic?"

"I'd bet my life on it. This had to have been painted by the Master. Of course, I will have to have my opinion corroborated by my boss, but there is no doubt in my mind this is a genuine Vermeer."

"As I thought," said Sandro. "But it wasn't dated."

"Only three of his works were," Hadley replied. She turned to face the prince.

"Prince Alessandro—um, Sandro—in researching provenance, I, as the investigator, try to produce a complete list of owners from the present time backward to when the painting left the artist's studio," Hadley explained. She knew that sometimes, especially in older paintings like the Vermeer in question, it was impossible to clarify a provenance definitively or to determine it was a work that came from a particular family and should be returned to the heirs of that family. This ambiguity kept companies like the Massimo Domingo Art Detective Agency in business.

"I may be able to help," Sandro said. "I just found this letter from my mother among her things, and I think it might answer some questions." He handed the fragile letter to Hadley.

Dear Sandro:

If you are reading this letter, your father and I are gone. I imagine you will be shocked to find Woman in Pearls and a Red Dress, a genuine Vermeer, in our possession. How do I know the painting is real when no one else seems to know a thing about it? That was intentional. We kept the secret for all these years. Now it's your turn to hear the story and keep the secret.

It was the end of the war, late April 1945. April 25, I remember, because it was our wedding anniversary. We were celebrating at home when there was a frantic knock on the door. Everyone knew the war was over and that the Germans, our former allies, were on the losing side. Italy was no longer under control of the Third Reich. Milan was not the stronghold it once was. Benito, or, as we called him, Il Duce, was to meet with a delegation of partisans at the palace of Cardinal Schuster. He told us that when he learned the Nazis had already begun negotiations for an unconditional surrender, he stormed out of the palace with Clara. That's Claretta Petacci, his mistress. They immediately fled Milan to Como, hoping to escape to Switzerland.

Your father and I had been friends with Mussolini, but things were beginning to get tenuous. People were turning on collaborators in a deadly way. Informers were everywhere, and the Italian people were bloodthirsty for revenge. The war was a mistake for Italy from the beginning, but we thought we were away from all the drama in Como. But Como is no different from the rest of the world. News travels fast. Especially bad news.

Il Duce begged us to take the painting for safekeeping. He knew we were art lovers and that we could be trusted, but I couldn't believe I was holding an authentic Vermeer. I almost dropped it, I was so nervous to realize I was holding in my trembling hands a work painted by the Master in the 1600s.

"Is th-this authentic?" I asked Il Duce.

"It's as real as you are standing in front of me, Principessa."

"Where did you get this?"

Benito's classic jaw tightened. "Courtesy of an exhibition in Rome. Later, I thought to bargain with Hitler for it. But I couldn't bear to part with it. The woman in the painting reminds you of my Clara, no? So beautiful in her red dress and pearls."

I looked at the frightened young woman by Benito's side. There was a resemblance, but the woman before me, the woman who shifted continuously, looking around like a caged animal, did not have the demeanor or the calm assurance of the subject of the painting. She couldn't wait to leave. I could hardly get a clear look at her face. She was afraid for her life and, as it turned out, she was right to be worried, since she had only three more days to live.

"We'll be back to collect it," Il Duce assured. "We're going to attempt to cross the border into Switzerland. From there, I don't know where we're headed, but hold on to this for me. Someone will be back to collect it. If I need to, I could use it later to bargain for our freedom or to sell. It's invaluable. No one is even aware of its existence, and if they are, they have no idea where it has been hidden all these years. I'm depending on you. Tell no one you have it. Though I know it will be tempting to show it off, to display it, don't give in to that urge. My enemies will get me any way they can."

He stared at the painting for a long time, hesitant to give it up, looking for a parting message, perhaps. Of course, your father and I promised. And we kept that promise all these years.

We invited them to stay the night, to have dinner at least, but they were in a hurry to move on. I have no idea where they spent the night, but the following day, they joined a convoy of fellow Fascists and German soldiers heading north toward the Swiss border.

So that was the last I saw of them, until of course we heard the news about their execution.

By now you know the story. According to historic accounts, Mussolini was wearing a German Luftwaffe helmet and overcoat, but the disguise did little to save him when partisans stopped the convoy at the lakeside town of Dongo on April 27. Mussolini was one of the most recognizable men on earth. With his shaved head and prominent jaw, his appearance gave him away.

The partisans seized Benito. Clara could have blended in with the crowd, but Benito inadvertently called attention to her by begging for special treatment for his mistress. The partisans hid the couple in a remote farmhouse overnight, afraid the Nazis would try to free him as they had done before. They weren't taking any chances.

The next morning, April 28, 1945, after enjoying their last evening together, unbeknownst to them, their last evening on earth, the partisans removed them from the house and drove them to the small village of Giulino di Mezzegra in northern Italy on the shores of Lake Como, not far from our villa. As the story goes, they were ordered to stand in front of a stone wall at the entrance to Villa Belmonte, where they were both executed by machine-gun fire. They say his killer was the communist partisan commander Walter Audisio.

Before dawn on April 29, the corpses of Mussolini, Petacci, and fourteen fellow Fascists were placed in a truck and dumped like so much garbage in Milan's Piazzale Loreto, the "Square of the Fifteen Martyrs." There was a reason they were taken to that place. Only eight months before, Fascists acting under order from the SS publicly had displayed the bodies of fifteen executed partisans. Now Mussolini and the others were put there also. Residents of Milan cursed him, threw vegetables at his corpse, kicked him, spat at him, and worse, beat his body beyond recognition and even fired more bullets into it. Then the crowd strung up the bodies at a gasoline station in the corner of the square. In early afternoon, American troops ordered the bodies to be taken down and Mussolini's corpse transported to the city morgue. I couldn't sleep for weeks after, imagining that it could happen to us. Oh, the nightmares. Every knock on the door had us frightened for our lives for years.

As the Soviets got closer to Berlin, apparently Hitler heard news of Mussolini's death. He didn't want to give his enemies the satisfaction of killing him in the same way, so he took the coward's way out and committed suicide on April 30.

Mussolini's body was buried in an unmarked grave in a Milan cemetery until Easter Sunday 1946, when Fascists dug it up, washed it in a nearby fountain, and pushed it in a wheelbarrow to a getaway car.

For nearly four months, the corpse was missing. It was found in August 1946, in the cupboard of a Capuchin monastery outside Milan. Once the Italian government recovered Mussolini's corpse, it kept its whereabouts secret for more than a decade. In 1957, the Italian prime minister finally delivered Mussolini's bones to his widow, where they received a burial in the family crypt.

With his death, we were powerless. The painting was cursed. Every time I look at it I see only the blood red of the dress and the deathly white of the translucent pearls. Yet it is so beautiful, I couldn't look away.

If anybody suspected we were hiding a Vermeer at the behest of Mussolini, they would have torn us limb from limb. Perhaps you've heard what they did to collaborators. We very well could have ended up like Il Duce and Clara. We had no idea if he had stolen it or where it came from, other than what he'd said. We even worried that Hitler knew of its existence and had charged one of his henchmen to retrieve it. Son, we literally lived in fear the rest of our lives.

Of course, we have regrets now about our relationship with Mussolini. But Il Duce was so confident, so charismatic, we were sure we would end up on the winning side.

We couldn't risk anyone finding out about the painting he left with us, no art dealer, no gossiper at a cocktail party. We waited, thinking that Mussolini may have given orders to someone—a criminal, a thief, a fencer, a buyer, a gallery owner—to collect the painting. But no one ever came, and there was no one we could safely approach. Even with all these years passed, I didn't know what to do or who to call or where to go. You'll have to decide what to do with the painting. My advice is to get rid of the thing at the first possible opportunity.

Love,
Mother

Hadley returned the letter, and the prince folded it up in its envelope.

"I had called an art dealer in Milan, Signore Bruno Lombardi, under the strictest confidence, to see if I could sell it or at least find out what it was worth. The taxes on this villa will put me into debt. That's why we're selling the place. But that was before I read my mother's letter. I'm afraid that word will spread, and I have to protect my parents' reputation, even after their death, although I am eager to get it off my hands and out of my life. Just make it go away. I don't want that stain on my family. And I don't want to be looking over my shoulder the rest of my life like my parents did."

"You did the right thing," Hadley assured. "Our agency will protect your identity. I can't vouch for the dealer, but I'm going to have a word with him before we go any further."

"He seemed very anxious to get his hands on the painting. He offered to come to the villa. In fact, we have an appointment scheduled for later today. I have dozens of other paintings that have been in my family for centuries that I want him to appraise."

"Good. That will give me a chance to meet him and size him up. He can't take the painting anywhere without your permission. Let me get my associate. Is there an office where I can set up my computer and do some research?"

"Of course," Sandro said, leading her down the hall to the library.

"This will do nicely," Hadley said.

"What are you going to do with the painting?"

"With your permission, I'd like to take it back to my boss for authentication," said Hadley. "I know in my heart and soul it's a Vermeer, but my boss is the expert. You have a lot of options. You could donate it to a museum. I could arrange a traveling exhibit that starts at the Uffizi and ends in the Rijksmuseum in Amsterdam."

"Is there any way to find out who it last legitimately

belonged to before Mussolini made off with it?"

"I'll continue doing research, but the benefit of a traveling exhibit is that someone might recognize it and step forward. Although, with a painting this valuable, I imagine a good many people will be stepping forward to press a claim. With all the publicity, we may be able to turn up the rightful owner."

"I'm just glad it will finally see the light of day so people can enjoy it. Do you think Mussolini left a trail of other paintings behind with other friends and loyalists?"

"It's highly possible."

While the prince went off to attend to business, Luca joined Hadley in the library.

"Did you learn anything?"

"Well, I'm no art expert, but there are a number of valuable-looking paintings packed in boxes down in the garage. Apparently, this guy is about to slip away with the loot."

"This is his house. Sandro says the artwork legitimately belongs to his parents."

"You are too trusting, Cara. I know human nature. You'd better take a look. I'll occupy the prince."

"How do you know they're valuable?"

"There are some nice-looking gold frames."

Hadley laughed. "You can't always judge a painting by its frame."

"That's why you're the art detective and I'm just an ordinary crime solver."

Hadley walked down a back staircase to the garage. There were a number of expensive-looking late-model sports cars, along with some artwork in packing crates. Luca was right. There was a treasure trove of paintings, all originals by the old Masters. Did they legitimately belong to the current owner? Or were they stolen?

In cases such as this one, where there were gaps in provenance, the first thing Hadley usually did was check with the Art Loss Register regarding stolen and disputed art and with the Lost Art Database for information on paintings which were removed and relocated, stored, or seized from their owners, particularly Jews, as a result of Nazi persecution and the consequences of World War II. Then she planned to contact her source at the FBI Stolen Art File. Of course, since she'd been working in Italy, she had developed an ongoing relationship with the Carabinieri Commando for the Protection of Cultural Heritage—or Art Squad, for short—the first and most important art police in the world. And Luca had a friend, an officer at the Art Squad, who would be a big help with the inquiry.

Hadley knew that most of the stolen art was Italian. Ten percent tended to be of foreign origin. After just a cursory search, she knew for a fact that many of these crated paintings belonged to Jewish families forced to sell at fire-sale prices just to survive or escape the Nazis. Had Sandro's parents been complicit in Il Duce's schemes all along? Her first duty was to solve the mystery of the vanished Vermeer. But she would not rest until she had the full story.

However, she and Luca couldn't just walk out with the crates. And what role did the art dealer play? Was he coming to pick up the artwork in the garage? Or was he solely focused on acquiring the Vermeer?

Back upstairs, Hadley was polite in her farewell. "Well, Sandro, it's been an honor to meet you. And thank you for trusting us with your painting."

Sandro caressed the ornate frame. "Well, she's not

really mine, is she?"

"But if it weren't for you, she never would have seen the light of day."

"She's a real beauty, isn't she?" he said with some regret. "It's hard to look away."

"I agree," said Luca, entering the room and staring intently at Hadley.

Hadley blushed as she returned his adoring look. "We're talking about *The Woman in Pearls and a Red Dress.*" Hadley's eyes wandered back to the painting on the easel, where it awaited the arrival of Signore Lombardi.

"To my mind, she's more compelling and enigmatic than the *Mona Lisa*. I wish I could have heard the conversation between the lady and the master while he was posing and painting her. And find out who she was. A lover, perhaps?"

"We'll never know," said Sandro.

The doorbell rang. Sandro went to greet Signore Lombardi and brought him into the solarium facing the lake.

"Hello, you must be Hadley Evans, Massimo's associate. I'm Signore Bruno Lombardi." He extended his hand. Hadley took it with a slight hesitation, but Luca refused the offer.

"And this is my associate, Luca Ferrari."

Signore Lombardi looked every part the villain—dark hair, with a neatly trimmed mustache, beady brown eyes, and a nervous laugh.

Luca inclined his head slightly while continuing to study the man under hooded lids. She could tell Luca didn't trust him. He was dissecting Signore Lombardi in his mind as though the man was an insect wriggling to escape from under a microscope. Luca had a refined sense of right and wrong. There were no gray areas.

"You were named after your father," Hadley noted to keep the conversation going.

"Yes," said the Signore, shifting uncomfortably under Luca's accusatory gaze. The dealer's father had a reputation, a bad one, and therefore the son was also suspect. During the war, the senior Lombardi had worked hand in hand with the Nazis, extorting valuable artwork from once-prosperous Jewish families who were homeless, desperate for money and a way out. And although he was tainted, he had escaped prosecution. Throughout the war, Jewish homes belonged to high-ranking party officials who admired the artwork on "their" walls. Some of those dispossessed were lucky enough to have escaped the concentration camps or survived the war, but most didn't return. Lombardi Senior considered he was doing a service for the Jews, helping them liquidate their assets before they themselves were liquidated. Was Signore Lombardi made from the same mold?

He cleared his throat. "My father died many years ago. I am now running the business. I was called by Prince Alessandro to assess some of his parents' paintings, one in particular, a Vermeer. I called your agency to verify the painting's authenticity. Have you seen it?"

"Yes," Hadley answered. "It almost certainly is the real thing, but Signore Domingo must authenticate it. We'll be taking it back to Florence with us."

"Certainly you don't need to do that, if you believe…"

"Signore," Hadley interrupted, "surely you are

aware that almost all of the inquiries we receive at our agency are junk or reproductions."

"Yes, but you said…"

"In my opinion. I have a sixth sense about authentic work. I have an art history background, yes, but to be absolutely sure, the painting will have to be officially appraised. Experts will study the brushwork…"

"But surely the date…"

"There is no date, which is typical of Vermeer, as you must surely know. Only three of his signed paintings were accompanied by dates. We will consult a curator at the Uffizi, who will be able to identify…"

"You are stalling," Signore Lombardi said, dropping all pretense. "Show me the painting," he demanded.

Luca's scowl tightened. He was on high alert. His hand instinctively moved to his hidden holster.

"Certainly," Hadley said, trying to lighten the tension. "It's right over here."

Prince Alessandro and Hadley led the dealer to the painting, with Luca on guard by the floor-to-ceiling windows.

When the Signore approached the painting, his hand flew to his throat.

"*Dio mio*, it is an original," he exclaimed.

No comment on the painting's beauty, the model's lifelike pose. Her compelling eyes. He did not appreciate this masterpiece. All he saw were dollar signs.

"We do not have a certificate of authentication," Hadley said. "And there is no record, no provenance for this particular painting."

She could tell the prince wanted to bring out the letter his mother had written, but she silenced him with her eyes.

"This could very likely be a better-than-adequate reproduction," Hadley posed.

"You'd have to be blind not to see this work is not a forgery. And it's worth a fortune."

"Prince Alessandro has agreed for us to borrow the painting and take it back to Florence to have it evaluated. Then it will be up to him as to what he wants to do with it."

"Prince Alessandro," Signore Lombardi pleaded, "we had an agreement, did we not?"

"I have some other very reputable works for you to look at in the garage. They're all bundled up and ready for you to take back to Milan to the gallery for sale."

"But the Vermeer." He turned on Hadley. "If it weren't for me contacting your boss, you wouldn't even know about the painting."

"That is true, but things have changed." At any moment, Hadley expected Signore Lombardi to break out in tears or attack them. She looked at Luca, who intuited her intent.

"Signore Lombardi," Luca said, placing his large hand firmly on the dealer's shoulder. "Please come with me. I believe we are finished here. The prince has changed his mind. You will not be representing him in any transaction."

Signore Lombardi knocked Luca's hand away roughly. "Who do you think you are?"

Luca inhaled. "I am with the Carabinieri in Florence, with close ties to the Art Squad. I'm sure if I called my associates, they would be very interested in paying you a visit in Milan to inspect your gallery. It would be a shame if they found any stolen art on the premises, or any art of questionable provenance."

The irate dealer stepped back but raised his fist. "You can't touch me. We are not in Florence."

Luca pulled out his Beretta 92 FS pistol. "As a Carabiniere, I have policing powers that I can exercise at any time and in any part of the country. And I have a very light trigger finger."

Luca was an imposing figure and could manifest a fierce attitude when it came to dispensing justice. There was no one else she trusted more. She was as sure as ever he would make a good life partner. Her cold feet were beginning to thaw.

"Don't hurt him, Detective," Hadley pleaded, smiling inwardly.

"He has nothing to worry about if he doesn't resist," Luca replied. He turned to Signore Lombardi and said evenly, "I will escort you to your car. But you will leave empty-handed. We can forget this incident ever happened."

Deflated, Signore Lombardi left the solarium with Luca's gun at his back.

"Would he really have used the gun?" the prince asked when they were out of sight.

"If he felt we were in danger, he would not have hesitated. You were the one who dodged a bullet, Your Highness, um, Sandro. That man was only in it for the profit. He didn't appreciate *her*." She inclined her head toward the painting.

"No," Sandro answered, staring longingly at the painting.

"I have a feeling we haven't seen the last of him," Hadley said. "But we'll deal with that later. For now, the *Woman in Pearls* is safe. Why don't you accompany us back to Florence? We'll rent a car and drive the paintings back to our offices. We will put you in touch with a reputable gallery who will get you the best price for your artwork, and we will see what we see with our *Woman in Pearls.*"

"You do think she's the real thing?"

"Absolutely."

"But what you said to Signore Lombardi…"

"To get him off the scent. He smelled money. He did not have your best interests at heart—or hers." Hadley crossed her arms in front of her. "It would be a shame to give up your beautiful villa. Perhaps with the profits you make on the paintings, you could afford to keep it."

"I would like nothing more."

"Then let's see if we can make that happen."

Chapter Twenty-Four

Rule Number Four: Use Your Mind To Paint The Essence Of A Problem As You Interpret It, In The Abstract.
~Massimo Domingo's Pocket Guide to Stolen Art Recovery—Volume 2

Back in Florence, the sun was shining. The church bells were ringing, and the wedding was only weeks away. But she was no closer to winning Luca's mother's stamp of approval than her parents were of warming up to her fiancé. She didn't have time to take a cooking course, and her Italian hadn't improved. All in all, in Signora Ferrari's opinion, she was a lost cause as daughter-in-law material. She wasn't Italian, and she couldn't cook. She would be expected to start producing babies exactly nine months after the wedding and stay home and raise them, but she wasn't ready to have children.

There was no way she was giving up her career. Massimo was thrilled that she had recovered the lost Vermeer. Experts had verified it was an original. Chunks of the provenance were missing, but since it had been in Mussolini's possession, odds are it had been stolen and the paperwork altered or destroyed. Hadley had arranged for the painting to be displayed at the Uffizi and then go on tour to museums across Europe. Her hope was that someone would recognize the painting and claim it.

Sandro had agreed to donate it anonymously, so Hadley had made the arrangements. No names were mentioned despite the fact that the Uffizi would have loved to honor the mysterious donor. Along with anonymity, the agreement included that the museum would never know how the painting had come into the hands of this particular donor. The Rossi family's reputation was protected. She had not even revealed the secret to Massimo, the publicity hound, who might have broadcast it at the first opportunity. It turned out that Sandro's parents had a houseful of Old Masters and other valuable paintings, legitimately acquired, so proceeds of the sale of that artwork allowed him to keep the villa in Cernobbio. She and Luca had a standing invitation to visit Lake Como.

Hadley's parents were due to arrive early to help her narrow down her choice of wedding dresses and finalize arrangements for the ceremony and reception. They were still stubbornly holding out hope that she would reunite with King Charles. That was never going to happen. Admittedly, she and Luca didn't have a lot in common. Yes, their backgrounds were very different, but she was convinced he was the one for her.

One member of Luca's family, his Italian Greyhound, Bocelli, on the other hand, was her greatest supporter. Around the house, Luca and Bocelli serenaded her with romantic arias. Well, Bocelli mostly howled, but they were adorable together. If she had Bocelli's approval, that was the only recommendation that meant anything to Luca.

Hadley was on her way back to the office when she passed a small ristorante—Antonio's—that she hadn't seen before. She walked into the establishment, lured by the most irresistible smells.

"Is this a new restaurant?" she asked the woman at the counter.

"Si. My husband and I just moved here from Capri. He was head chef at one of the resorts there, and when the owner decided to open a restaurant in Florence, Antonio volunteered to run it. It's a great opportunity for us. Our daughter lives in Florence, so we were happy to come."

"Welcome to Florence."

"You're not Italian."

"How did you guess?"

"Your Southern accent gave you away."

Hadley laughed. "That's turning out to be a big problem for me."

"Why?"

"My fiancé's mother was hoping for an Italian daughter-in-law who could cook. She got a Southern belle who can't boil water. I have a feeling no woman would be good enough for her son."

"I'm Gina, by the way," said the woman, extending her hand.

Hadley shook it warmly. "I'm Hadley Evans. I work right around the corner at the Massimo Domingo Art Detective Agency. Do you have any take-out menus or business cards I can pass out? I'll put the word out about your new place and help you drum up some business. The food smells great."

"It tastes great, too. Antonio is a wizard in the kitchen," said Gina. "He makes the best red sauce in Italy. Come, sit down. I'll bring you a bowl of pasta."

Hadley took the offered seat, and within minutes she

was savoring the best spaghetti sauce she'd ever tasted. Better than Luca's mother's recipe.

"Oh, my God, this is amazing," Hadley said. "I wish I could cook pasta sauce this good. My wedding is in a few weeks. Do you think you could cater the wedding luncheon? We've already made arrangements for the dinner."

"We'd love to. Let me get the date on my calendar."

"That would be wonderful."

"Hadley, I suddenly had a great idea. What if I got Antonio to give you cooking lessons? If we work hard together, by the time of the wedding, you can impress your mother-in-law with your culinary talents."

"Gina, that's wonderful. I'd be so grateful."

"The first lesson will be to learn to boil water. Then Antonio will teach you all his secrets."

Chapter Twenty-Five

Rule Number Five: Use A Free Hand When Approaching A Problem. Sometimes it's necessary to bend the rules and seek a *fresco* (ha-ha) approach.
~Massimo Domingo's Pocket Guide to Stolen Art Recovery—Volume 2

Every morning, before work, Hadley dropped by Antonio's to help prepare the food for the day. She returned during lunch to help with the noontime rush and again in the evening to learn and lend a hand in the kitchen. In short order, she learned to make various kinds of pasta from scratch and a variety of sauces. By the time she got home, she dropped into bed, exhausted. Luca was getting suspicious about her absences and her excuses for canceling their plans.

"Why can't you go out with me anymore?" She could sense Luca's frustration over the telephone. "Every night it's a different excuse. You have to prepare for the wedding. You have to work late. You have an errand to run. When I offer to help, you turn me down. Is something wrong?"

"Nothing is wrong. We're very busy at work."

"At ten o'clock at night? I've been by the office, and it's closed. Where do you go every night? Have you changed your mind about the wedding?"

"No, of course not," Hadley assured him. "It's a

surprise, so I can't tell you, but it will make you and your mother very happy."

"What does my mother have to do with it?"

"You'll find out soon."

"I miss you. Bocelli misses you, too."

"I miss you both too. But we'll have plenty of time together after the wedding. I've got to go. Love you."

In her free time, she practiced making the dishes at home. Her parents were flying in tomorrow, so she would have to spend time with them, and there was a lot to do before the wedding. At least the food was taken care of. She and Gina had planned a great wedding luncheon menu.

Chapter Twenty-Six

Rule Number Six: No Matter What The Medium Of A Missing Masterpiece, The Same Rules Of Engagement Apply In Tracking It Down.
~Massimo Domingo's Pocket Guide to Stolen Art Recovery—Volume 2

Hadley was dead on her feet. She'd already put in an early morning at Antonio's, learning his culinary secrets and helping out in the restaurant however she could, to thank them for their generosity. And she had done an evening shift the night before. When she walked into the office, Gerda sprang out of her seat and confronted her.

"Where have you been? I've been calling you. Massimo is furious."

"At me?"

"No, not at you. But we've been trying to find you. What's that smell? You smell like spaghetti sauce."

Hadley thought she'd showered and washed off the smell of red sauce. "What is he so hyped up about?"

"The Vermeer. It's gone. Someone broke into the warehouse last night and stole it."

"What?" Hadley exclaimed. This was the worst possible news.

"But the warehouse is guarded."

"Whoever stole it overpowered them, and when they

came to, the Vermeer was gone."

"What about the other paintings?"

"Apparently the thief was only interested in the Vermeer."

"But we promised it to the Uffizi for the exhibition. It's due to be transferred there at the end of the week. The exhibition starts Monday. People have already bought tickets. How could this have happened?"

"That's what Massimo wants to know. Uh-oh. Here he comes now." Gerda hurried back to her desk to avoid the fallout.

"Hadley, have you heard the news? The Vermeer has vanished!"

"Gerda filled me in. Have you called in the Carabinieri Art Squad?"

"Yes. They've been through our warehouse looking for leads. But who knows how long the painting will take to find! Every day the painting is missing decreases the odds that we will ever find it. The thief probably already has a buyer lined up—a museum, a major auction house, another well-known dealer, or a private collector. The painting could be on its way out of the country by now. Once it's smuggled out, we may never recover it. And even if we trace it, the buyer will likely refuse to return it. What will we tell the Uffizi? I'm sure the newspapers will have a field day! I can see the headlines now. *Massimo Domingo lets another Vermeer slip through his fingers.* The exhibition is next week."

"You didn't lose it. And you had nothing to do with the theft of the Vermeer in Boston."

"But I couldn't find it. My name will be forever associated with missing Vermeers."

"Calm down. I'm going to get her back. I have an

idea where she might be. I'm going to—"

"No, you're not going to do anything. It's too dangerous. Whoever stole the painting has already injured two guards."

"I'm going to alert Luca. He's a professional."

"What's that smell?" Massimo asked. "I'm getting hungry. I'm going down to Antonio's. Can I bring anyone back anything?"

Gerda shook her head. "It's the middle of the morning. Didn't you just eat breakfast?"

"I can't focus on an empty stomach," Massimo replied.

"I may be gone for a day or two," Hadley said.

"Whatever it takes. Just don't take any unnecessary chances."

"I won't. But Luca and I will track her down."

"Aren't your parents coming in tomorrow?" Gerda said.

"Yes. If I'm not back by tomorrow night, can you keep them occupied?"

"Sure."

Hadley called Luca.

"Can you come over to the office right away? We have an emergency."

"Are you all right?"

"Yes, but the Vermeer has been stolen."

"I'll be right over. It seems like weeks since I've seen you. I'll get my sister to watch Bocelli."

When Luca arrived at the office, he wrapped her in his arms and pressed her against his body. Then he held her back and began sniffing her. "Cara, you smell delicious. Is that a new perfume? It's making me hungry for….pasta, among other things."

Hadley sighed. Apparently, she was going to smell like tomato sauce for the rest of her life.

"It's Eau de Pomodoro," Hadley joked. "Gerda, we're going to run down to the station and catch the next train to Milan. Could you book us a hotel there?"

"Sure. But what about clothes?"

"If we need a change, we'll buy some there. It's the fashion capital of the world."

Luca looked like he could swallow her whole. He took in a breath. "Cara. *A hotel. No clothes.*"

"Luca, this is business. We won't have time to see the inside of the hotel room."

Luca frowned.

Hadley grabbed his hand. "Come on, we don't have any time to lose."

"Why are we going to Milan?"

"Remember that smarmy art dealer from Milan, Signore Lombardi, who came to the Villa Rossi? He was very interested in the Vermeer. I'll bet he stole it and took it back to his gallery and is hiding it there or in a warehouse or at his home, waiting for a buyer."

"I never trusted him. Do we have a home address for the guy?"

"It was in that original packet Massimo gave me, but I've asked Gerda to text it to me."

"Shouldn't I alert the Carabinieri to surround his gallery or get a search warrant for his house?"

"That will overwhelm him. It might scare him away. Let's just the two of us go to the gallery first and see what's up. But yes, they can arrange for a search warrant and be waiting for us before they raid his warehouse. That's a good idea. Don't they have about three hundred agents?"

"Yes, and their database contains information about more than a million stolen objects."

"Who knows what else we'll find there? You know there are solid rumors that his father was working with Hitler and Mussolini to move stolen art from museums across the continent. If we can confirm some of the dealer's artwork was stolen, we might have enough for a Recovered Treasures exhibit. But right now, I want to focus on the Vermeer. We have to get her back."

When Hadley and Luca arrived at Santa Maria Novella station, she bought two tickets on the next train to Milan's Centrale station. Luckily, the train was a high-speed direct that would get them into Milan in one hour and fifty minutes. Much better than the typical journey of three hours and five minutes. There were twenty-three direct trains from Florence to Milan each day.

She and Luca settled in seats across from each other in Executive Class service. The flagship red arrow train was comfortable and ultra-modern, with access to a gourmet meal served at their seats. Luca moved over to the seat next to her.

"What are you doing?"

"I can't kiss you if you're way over there."

"Luca, people will be sitting in the seats next to us."

"I don't see any people, do you?"

"Not yet, but—"

Luca silenced her with a slow, amorous kiss. "We only have an hour and fifty minutes on this journey. Let's see what mischief we can get up to."

"You're impossible," Hadley said, returning his kisses, then coming up for air, adding, "We have to discuss wedding plans."

"First things first," Luca said, holding her tighter

against his body.

The train began to move, and she nestled in Luca's arms, kissing him as the train pulled out of the station. They seemed to be alone in the cabin.

"Put your hand down there," Luca coaxed as the train gained momentum. She felt his weapon.

"Why do you want me to feel your gun?"

He moved her hand lower. "That's not what I had in mind, Cara."

Chapter Twenty-Seven

Rule Number Seven: A Contemporary Canvas May Be No Less Valuable Than A Fifteenth-Century Work Of Art If You Peel Back The Layers. Restoration works wonders. True beauty is a *pigment* of your imagination. Open yourself to a palette of possibilities.
~*Massimo Domingo's Pocket Guide to Stolen Art Recovery—Volume 2*

The Comando Carabinieri Tutela Patrimonio Culturale (TPC) is in the business of safeguarding and protecting Italy's rich art history. Hadley had no doubt they would do their job. But the Vermeer had disappeared under her watch, and she wanted to be the one to get it back. Perhaps they were chasing shadows in Milan, but her instincts told her she was on the right track. The dealer was the only other person who knew about the Vermeer besides the prince. And he was anxious to get rid of the painting. It might have been a coincidence that the Vermeer was stolen, but Hadley didn't believe in coincidences.

Signore Lombardi wouldn't have stolen it himself. He'd probably sent some lackeys to do his dirty work. By now, the masterpiece would be at his residence or in his gallery or his warehouse.

Hadley and Luca checked into the hotel, freshened up, and walked to the nearby gallery in Centro Storico.

It was one o'clock, so the gallery was closed for the midday riposa and wouldn't open again until 3:30 p.m.

"He wouldn't be stupid enough to keep the painting here, in the obvious place."

"I agree."

"Do you have the address of his warehouse?" Hadley asked.

"Yes, my friend in the Art Squad got it for me. Signore Lombardi's father has been on their screen for a long time."

"Their screen? Oh, you mean on their radar."

"Si. I've been in contact with them. They're checking the warehouse now."

"Then let's pay him a visit at his home. I have that address." Hadley hailed a taxi from outside the hotel lobby and handed them a piece of paper with the address. "It's on the outskirts of Milan, near Bergamo."

Hadley and Luca were quiet in the taxi. When the car pulled into the circular driveway of an exclusive, three-story eighteenth-century villa, surrounded by a well-tended park with a river flowing nearby, Hadley's eyes widened. An impressive fountain stood outside a Mediterranean golden-yellow stucco façade with turquoise-trimmed windows. She asked the taxi driver for his number and paid him extra for his availability. "We'll call you when we're ready to return to Milan."

"Business must be good," Luca observed, exiting the cab and helping Hadley out.

"I'll say. This place is a palace. I looked him up on the Internet. This house was just renovated. Renovations cost money. There are twenty-five bedrooms!"

"Why does he need all that space?"

"He rents it out for events and ceremonies," Hadley

said.

Luca used the ornate brass door knocker to signal their arrival.

A tall, uniformed man answered the door.

"May I help you?"

"We're looking for Signore Bruno Lombardi," Hadley announced.

"Do you have an appointment?" he asked.

"No, but we're here on police business," Luca added, flashing his badge.

The butler raised his brows but maintained a polite air.

"The Signore is at his gallery. I'm expecting him home soon. If you'd like, you may wait. Follow me. Would you like some refreshment?"

"That would be wonderful," Hadley said.

The butler led them into a large state hall, a lavish space adorned with refined Neoclassical collections, Venetian terrazzo floors, and ceilings frescoed by painters Hadley recognized.

"I'm going to have a look around some of these twenty-five bedrooms before the butler gets back," Luca said.

"Be careful. Don't get lost."

"Cara," said Luca with a deadpan expression, "don't miss me too much."

Several minutes later, the butler returned with a silver tray of fruits, cheeses, and pastries and placed it on a table in front of her.

"This is lovely, thank you," Hadley said.

"Where is your friend?"

"He had to use the restroom. I understand there are ten of them."

"That is correct. He's been gone quite a long time."

"It must have been something he ate on the train to Milan that disagreed with him."

The butler looked doubtful. "I'll let you know when the Signore returns."

"I appreciate that," said Hadley covering her lap with a folded white napkin.

Twenty minutes later, Luca reappeared.

"Where have you been," Hadley hissed. "Lurch is beginning to get suspicious."

"Who is this Lurch?"

"Never mind."

"I had a look around, and you won't believe what I found."

"What?"

"The Vermeer. Hiding in plain sight."

"Tell me. Where?" Hadley jumped up excitedly, grabbing Luca's arms.

"I wandered into another state hall and the room looked like it was set up for an auction. There were about twenty chairs lined up, with a podium, a microphone, a gavel, and a TV hook-up, I guess for the out-of-towners who couldn't gather in person. The Vermeer was hidden under a cloth on an easel, waiting to be revealed."

"You just took the painting?"

"Well, actually, I removed a similar-sized painting on the wall and substituted it for the Vermeer. It's hidden under a cloth, so no one will notice until the auction begins."

"Clever. Where is she now?"

She's hiding in the bushes out front.

"Hiding in the bushes?"

"Yes. I called the taxi, and when he meets us out

front, I'll grab the painting, and we'll be on our way."

"But what about the Signore?"

"Let's let the Art Squad deal with him. Animals like that are dangerous when they're cornered. There's an arrest warrant out for the man. I got a call from my contact, and they found a warehouse full of stolen art, paintings that disappeared during World War Two. Everything is well documented. The names and addresses of families the art was confiscated from and the provenance of the paintings. Who the paintings were sold to. These are masterpieces the Art Squad has been trying to track down for decades. Apparently, Lombardi Senior represented both Mussolini and Hitler, and first he and now his son have been trading off ill-gotten gains illicitly all these years. No wonder Lombardi Junior can live like a king in this villa, up to his throat in the dirty business."

Hadley laughed. "You mean up to his neck."

"Like I said. You and Massimo will have your hands full, repatriating all of that stolen Nazi art."

The butler entered the room.

"Signore Lombardi has been delayed. And we're about to have company, so I'm afraid you'll have to leave."

"Thank you for the refreshments," Hadley said. "Everything was delicious."

"Who shall I say was calling?"

Hadley looked at Luca.

"Never mind. We'll be back in touch."

The butler walked them to the door, and they started for the cab. When the door closed, Luca recovered the painting from behind the bushes, wrapped in a towel he had taken from one of the ten bathrooms, and handed it to Hadley, who was already seated in the cab.

Hadley admired the masterpiece. "I will never get tired of looking at her. It's her eyes. She draws you in."

"She is beautiful," Luca admitted, "but not as beautiful as you."

"I would give anything to see the look on Signore Lombardi's face when he removes the cloth from the easel and finds his Vermeer missing," Hadley said.

"No doubt the Art Squad will interrupt the proceedings just in time."

Chapter Twenty-Eight

Rule Number Eight: If It Ain't Baroque, Don't Fix It. You may choose to pursue more modern methods, but don't discount the tried-and-true techniques.

~*Massimo Domingo's Pocket Guide to Stolen Art Recovery—Volume 2*

Massimo was on top of the world. His reputation was restored. The Vermeer was safely at the Uffizi, being enjoyed by thousands of patrons at the exhibition. Her boss had taken most of the credit for the monumental discovery, but he had "generously" shared some of the spotlight with Hadley.

They had their work cut out for them returning the dozens of stolen paintings to their rightful owners or the heirs of those owners. She wasn't going to miss out on that adventure. Newspapers around the world were reporting on the spectacular cache of stolen art found in Signore Lombardi's warehouse and his dark ties with the past. He would be in prison for a long time.

The sun shone bright on her wedding day. She and Luca were all smiles during the ceremony, lost in each other and their happiness. Hadley's parents looked like they'd just swallowed something distasteful. Luca's mother looked like she'd rather be anywhere else, her mouth puckered like she'd just sucked on a lemon. The front row on both sides of the aisle wore expressions more suitable to a funeral than a wedding. The frowns did not bode well for the wedding pictures.

After the ceremony, the group gathered at Antonio's to celebrate at the wedding luncheon.

"This red sauce is delicious sauce," exclaimed Luca's mother.

"That's your new daughter-in-law's secret recipe," Gina said. "She's an excellent chef."

Hadley winked at her co-conspirator, Gina.

Luca's mother looked at Hadley in surprise, and her expression softened.

"Of course, it's not as good as mine," she said.

"Of course not," Hadley graciously agreed.

"I didn't know you could cook," Luca whispered.

"There's a lot you don't know about me," Hadley replied, eyes twinkling.

"I can't wait to find out," Luca said, smiling broadly.

A word about the author…

Born in Miami, Florida, Marilyn Baron is a public relations consultant in Atlanta and a member of Atlanta Writers Club. She writes in a variety of genres, from Women's Fiction to Historical Romantic Thrillers and Romantic Suspense to Paranormal Fantasy and has won writing awards in single title, suspense romance, novel with strong romantic elements, and paranormal/fantasy romance.

She was the Finalist in the 2017 Georgia Author of the Year (GAYA) Awards in the Romance category for her novel *Stumble Stones* and the Finalist for the 2018 GAYA Awards in the Romance category for her novel *The Alibi*.

Her new novel, *The Case of the Missing Botticelli*, is her 27th work of fiction. She is past chair of Roswell Reads and serves on the Atlanta Author Series Committee. She graduated from The University of Florida in Gainesville, Florida, with a Bachelor of Science in Journalism and a minor in Creative Writing.

Inspired by her six months spent studying in college in Florence, Italy, and the many times she's visited Italy on business or vacation, she set this new cozy mystery series in Firenze.

To find out more about her books, please visit her Web site at www.marilynbaron.com.

Thank you for purchasing
this publication of The Wild Rose Press, Inc.

For questions or more information
contact us at
info@thewildrosepress.com.

The Wild Rose Press, Inc.
www.thewildrosepress.com